IF WISHES WERE OBFUSCATION CODES
AND OTHER STORIES

MALON EDWARDS

Fireside
FICTION COMPANY

Boston, Mass.

Editor: Brian J. White
Copy editor: Sydnee Thompson
Proofreader: Johanie Martinez-Cools
Book designer: CreativeJay
Cover illustrator: Alexxander Dovelin
Cover designer: Frank Cvetkovic

Published by Fireside Fiction Company
Boston, Mass.

Firesidefiction.com
EBOOK ISBN: 978-1-7341549-8-6
PRINT ISBN: 978-1-7341549-9-3

To my sister, Mia, who introduced me to science fiction when she saw my drawings of planets and their written entries copied from an astronomy guidebook.

To my wife, Anne, whose ingenuity, wit, charm, and impressive ideas make me want to be a better writer every day.

Foreword

I love world-building.

Twelve years ago, I became a permanent resident of Canada, lured here by my beautiful wife, Anne. I can't remember if I heard "Brown Girl in the Ring" at a birthday party Anne and I attended before I read Nalo Hopkinson's *Brown Girl in the Ring*, but at that party, watching the reverie unfold I felt something *unfamiliar*. Like *something* was missing.

The Greater Toronto Area is truly multicultural. Anne is Hungarian-Japanese and most of her friends are an equally rich blending of ethnicities. West Indian Indian. West Indian Black. West Indian Black Asian. Middle Eastern Maritime.

All of them are complete and engaged in their diversity. They slipped so smoothly between their respective histories, their languages—an intricate, joyous, and very loud! mashing of English and a myriad of dialects that was completely natural. It was beautiful.

I wished I had that.

That party, that song, that true melting pot in my new home country—and being a Black Chicagoan in that moment—left me with a new kind of yearning, a desire to belong I couldn't quite articulate.

My mother's side of the family is from Mississippi, and many (many!) live in New Orleans. There's always been talk of the uniqueness of the Creole culture there, and of really, *really* unique people. True characters. People and culture I wanted to put into my stories.

But, as any truly good-and-shy writer would do, I chose not to call my family to mine information from them. I didn't ask questions or take notes over a pot of jambalaya with Uncle Role or Antie Annette or Aunt Cute, or unreservedly dig into the lore of my kin. Nope.

Instead, I started quietly world-building a fictional culture in an alt-Chicago with elements of Louisiana Creole. (Somehow, my introverted logic fully conceded this would be easier, even though some of my older cousins shared bits of our Creole heritage.)

In 2009, I found very little Louisiana Creole online, save one limited Louisiana Creole dictionary. Not-so-coincidentally, one of my main dark fantasy characters at the time, Bijou LaVoix, was forbidden to speak Louisiana Creole by her mother. In the story, it was because her English grades weren't good enough. In reality, I couldn't figure out how to realistically weave in and do justice to that distinct and distant tongue in my writing.

I continued to search for good Louisiana Creole resources, and then, one day I had the incredibly good fortune to find Mandaly Louis-Charles's blog, Sweet Coconuts, for Haitian Creole. I was astounded by the amount of information, depth, and detail. It was a thrilling discovery, one I'd been waiting for, even though it was a different kind of Creole.

Immediately, I shifted my world-building.

My stories that followed were set in an alt-Chicago where the real Jean Baptiste Point du Sable, thought to have been born in Haiti, still founded Chicago, but didn't leave to trade. No, in my world, he became Chicago's lord mayor and established Haitian Creole as its official language. He made the city obscenely rich through its minerals, pissed off the State of Illinois by hoarding the wealth, and seceded Chicago from Illinois to make it a sovereign state. In my alt-Chicago, Jean Baptiste was THE MAN. He raised up my birth-city as the black market capital and technological center of America.

To expand my world, many of these stories incorporated elements of my life, including characters based on my mother and her sisters. And her brothers. And my grandfather. And my grandmother, Big Mama.

My mama was one of twelve, so there were personalities aplenty. And there were characters who mirrored my half sister. My biological father. My step father, who's my chosen dad. My four step brothers, who are my blood brothers.

I'd eventually realize I had a connection—many connections—all along. I'd just overlooked them.

I wrote every story with this thick, deep background in mind, especially the ones in this collection. I also tried my best to accurately incorporate some of the Haitian Creole language and grammar from the Sweet Coconuts blog. Though, I often asked myself if this was cultural appropriation, while always, *always* feeling an enormous cultural appreciation as I continued to learn more.

Two years ago, I was invited to be part of a Caribbean Diaspora writers panel. The invite itself was a heady experience; two deeply respected authors, one of whom I'd long, long admired, had come up with the idea that I should be offered a place on said distinguished stage. The writer who extended the invite said she loved my Half Dark stories in *Shimmer* magazine. The other, much to my elated (somewhat starstruck) inner fanboy ego, mentioned I would be a good fit. I was tremendously flattered and said so, but declined the panelist offer. Somehow, I felt it would've been wrong to participate.

I was just as flattered (and enormously grateful) when I asked Mandaly Louis-Charles to narrate one of my stories, "Shadow Man, Sack Man, Half Dark, Half Light," and she said my Haitian Creole was "on point." Coming from her, it was the highest compliment.

I wasn't (and still am not) proficient in Haitian Creole, though. Mandalay took the time to make linguistic corrections on other stories she agreed to narrate for me (for *Escape Pod* and *PodCastle*), which I wholeheartedly appreciate.

So, my Haitian Creole isn't perfect. And my writing isn't perfect. Neither is my world-building.

But it is a meticulously crafted labor of love.

I hope you enjoy reading these stories as much as I enjoyed writing— and building—them.

Malon Edwards

Better Than Everything

"So, I've been thinking," I start, and then stop because this is the conversation we've been avoiding most of her life.

But Jae Lyn doesn't miss a beat. "You keep doing that, and you're going to break something."

She smiles, and that dimple at the left corner of her mouth peeks out at me. More than anything, I'll miss kissing it.

No. I can't think like that.

I take a carton of apple-cranberry juice out of the refrigerator, pour us both a glass, and proceed to wipe that smile right off her face.

"You can't die."

"Don't."

"We have to talk about this."

"No. We have to go to prom."

"You won't make it to prom." I look at my watch. It's just after five-thirty in the afternoon. "Prom starts at nine. How much time do you have left? Three hours?"

"Sixteen."

"Liar."

"I'm the gynoid," Jae Lyn says. "I should know."

"Turn around."

She looks up at me. I've never seen this Jae Lyn cry in the eleven months I've known her, but I swear she's about to right now. She turns around, though. Probably to hide her tears.

I lift her black bebe T-shirt to her shoulder blades and press my index finger to the base of her neck. Digital numbers glow red on the middle of her back beneath her smooth, golden brown skin: 02:56:47.

And counting.

Shit.

0 0 0

Jae Lyn was fourteen when she died from brain cancer. Nobody saw it coming. She'd been healthy that Christmas, just months before.

She got sick fast. I couldn't deal with her pain. She was my first love. My only love. But I just couldn't go visit her in the hospital.

We'd been going together for about a year when she was diagnosed—mainly just holding hands and kissing. Nobody knew, except for Matty. He helped me and Jae Lyn live our lie. For her parents. For my mama.

But we helped him out, too. Highland Park's most gifted football player ever is supposed to have a girlfriend, not a boyfriend.

Me and Matty were the perfect power-athlete couple. We still are. Matty and Zakiya. Star quarterback and state champion high jumper. Should have been Jae Lyn and Zakiya.

Jae Lyn had been strong. Beautiful. A kickass athlete. ESPN had projected her to finish her debut year ranked 87th by the Women's Tennis Association, the highest-ranked Filipina in the world. I was so proud of her. But I just could not bring myself to see her wasting away like that.

I wanted to remember her as I'd always known her: as the phenom who was about to make some serious noise on the pro tennis circuit. As the girl who loved me for me. Despite my name. Despite my dark skin. Despite my lean height.

And yet, I wasn't there for her.

That's my biggest regret. Making it all about me and not about Jae Lyn. I told myself she'd get better. That I'd be there for her after she got out of the hospital. That I'd help her get sexy-strong again. Work out with her. Like we used to.

We never did. On Valentine's Day she was dead.

0 0 0

"Blanford Sutton gives each of you a bioelectric battery with a calendar life of about a year, right?" I pull Jae Lyn's shirt back down and slip my arms around her waist. She leans her head back against my chest.

"I figure it runs on the keratin in your synth hair and the collagen in your synth skin."

"How do you figure that?"

"Google. Wikipedia."

She half-laughs, half-sobs. "I don't have a chance."

I hug her tight. "Listen. In about two hours, your skin is going to wrinkle up and dry out. Your hair is going to get brittle and break off."

"You don't know that for sure."

"It happens all the time. It happened to a gynoid in Sweden. I saw it on YouTube. But then I saw her skin and hair come back."

Jae Lyn takes my arms from around her and places my hands over where her heart should be. "You sound like you have a plan."

"I do." I put my face in her neck and take in her wonderful sweet pea scent. "There's this rumor going around the internet that Stanford Sutton and Blanford Sutton's little brother, Manford Sutton, put an Easter egg in the software for your battery to make it last longer."

She turns to face me again. "I hear a 'but' coming." Her eyes shimmer. Two big, fat tears plop onto the tile floor. I don't care what Mama says. Jae Lyn is a seventeen-year-old girl through and through.

"But—" My face goes hot. I reach up and play with my newly done-up Bantu knots. "Supposedly, the Easter egg is a combination of fructose, lipids, and proteolytic enzymes."

I talk fast, afraid Jae Lyn might interrupt me. Or worse, fall out on the floor laughing.

"Some people think energy from the combination can power your battery. Make it go further. I don't know how much more time it would give you. No one has figured that out yet. But I swear to you it works, and I'll prove it. I'm going to see Maddie Nice and wait 'til you see what I bring back."

0 0 0

I've known Maddie Nice since seventh grade. We met at a summer program for smart kids.

I remember it like it was yesterday. She'd asked me about Azure Yeast. I asked her if that was a new ice cream flavor. She just grinned at me and started singing one of their songs. It sounded familiar. I'd heard it on the radio.

We gravitated toward one another and became fast best friends back then. We still are. We know each other's hopes. Each other's fears. Each other's misery.

But knowing all that about her didn't make it any easier—or less awkward—when I asked her for a small box of her Purple Rain lip gloss earlier today. For free.

I mean, why not? I've put in my time. I tell you for days about the chemical ingredients of Purple Rain because she went on about them to me for months. I can recite them in my sleep, which I have done (ask my mama), along with what they can do to gynoids and androids.

So, I know Purple Rain like I know my big, beautiful lips. I've been using that lip gloss for two months now, and I swear to you before God and all that is holy: My lips are two years younger than the rest of my body, organs included. Maddie Nice did that.

You should've seen her face. For a split second, it was all displeasure and anger. Her face said I should know better. She's a fifth-class chemist. She couldn't afford to give her product away for free, especially when Manford Sutton has it on a six-month back order for the Electric Resurrected he likes best. I'd truly hurt her feelings, but then her face softened and she became her namesake when she thought I was going to cry. I wasn't. Or maybe I was. But that was because I knew Jae Lyn only had a few more hours to live, and she was wasting time being mad at me.

When I told Maddie what I needed her Purple Rain lip gloss for and how many hours I thought Jae Lyn had left, she moved with the quickness. As long as I've known her, I could always count on Maddie Nice.

She unlocked a wall panel behind her and took out a big box.

"I don't need that much," I told her, trying to be polite.

She smiled and handed it to me. "You and I both know you do. Tell me you've finished that one lip gloss I gave you. Now tell me you want Jae Lyn to use just one lip gloss like you do. I know you don't. Spoil her, Zakiya. Make her battery last as long as you and she want."

"Thank you." I kissed her on the cheek. "I owe you," I told her as I ran out her shop.

"Damn right you do!" she called after me in the doorway. How could I not? Back when me and Maddie were missing curfew left, right, and center, Mama used to say I had trouble in one back pocket and Maddie in the other.

Truth is, she ain't never lied. Maddie Nice kept trouble as far away from me as she could.

0 0 0

Jae Lyn is quiet and still for so long I think her bio-clock was wrong and she's already wound down for good. But finally she whispers, "I'm ready to die."

I act like I don't hear her. "Some people also think Blanford Sutton did this on purpose. That he gave you a short battery life and no self-preservation program because he knows wealthy, grieving parents will just order another daughter."

I grab her tight again and mumble into her cool-as-hell, dark pixie hair. "Parents are forever sad, Blanford Sutton is forever rich, and people like me are forever forgotten."

"Age progression and memory upgrades are free," she says. "I'll remember you."

She didn't before. Not at first. I was lucky Jae Lyn had some residual memories of me tucked away with our workouts.

The worst thing that has ever happened to me was when Jae Lyn came back from the dead in our sophomore year. I'd found her alone outside the girls' locker room after tennis practice. Gave her the sexiest kiss I could muster. And she pushed me away. Hard. Because she didn't know me.

Jae Lyn and I figure her parents finally got a clue two versions ago, so they told Blanford Sutton to remove all her memories of me. Especially of us together.

That must have cost them crazy money. Probably took Blanford Sutton's coders until the cows came home, as Mama would say. But they'd done a half-assed job of it.

The phone rings. It's Jae Lyn's parents. They've found us. Again.

I can tell they've been crying, even though the holo-screen over the kitchen island is dim with don't-answer mode. I reach to activate it.

"Don't." Jae Lyn squeezes me tight. "I want to spend my last few hours with you. Not them."

She stands on her tiptoes and kisses me in that special way of hers. All fluttery. My lips tingle. She's always liked my full lips.

My face gets hot again. "We should try."

"My parents have already filled out the paperwork. Don't worry. I'll be back next week."

I take her by the hand. "I'd like to try," I whisper. "Don't you?" Before she can answer, I speak in a rush. "What if they order brand-new memory specs? Or tell Blanford Sutton to find the rest of me and rip that out of you?"

Jae Lyn shakes her head. "They won't."

"I can't go through this again." I try to keep the desperation out of my voice. And fail. "I really want to do this now. But I won't make you. I want you to want this. I mean, who knows how much more time this would give you?"

Jae Lyn leads me to the bottom of the stairs. "Who knows what it would *do* to me? I mean, this is just some crazy internet bio-hack, right?"

"You do want to save yourself, don't you?"

Jae Lyn places her palms flat against my back and lays her head on my chest. "I just want to listen to your heartbeat."

This is the third time in three years I've heard a version of her say that to me. And the third time I wait for one of her to die in my arms. Lately, I've been a sucker for her dying requests.

My vision blurs with tears. I can't do this again. I don't want to do this again.

"Why did you lead me here if you don't want to save yourself?" My voice is a whisper.

"Come on." Jae Lyn pulls me up the stairs.

I let out a shaky breath. I'm not ready to smile yet.

I refuse to serve continued penance for my past mistakes. I refuse to hold her again as she winds down for good.

I refuse to hope against hope for at least one more year with another one of her. For a Jae Lyn who remembers me. For a Jae Lyn who loves me. For a Jae Lyn who doesn't push me away.

Not this time. Not a year from now. Not ever again.

0 0 0

We don't speak as I open the box. Our eyes look everywhere but at each other. I move fast, and not just because Jae Lyn has less than three hours of life. I have that tight, fluttery feeling inside.

It's not often I get to have a first with my girlfriend again.

Goosebumps make me feel even tighter, so I run to the bed, throw the covers over my head, and curl up into a ball. My teeth won't stop chattering. I want Jae Lyn to spoon me.

And then she does.

I want time to stop. I want to stay like that forever.

"I remember this." Her breath is *warm* on my shoulder.

I don't want Jae Lyn to see my smile. I don't want her to like this, as much as it feels so right. I'm all long angles and elbows, and she's all tight and curvy, but we'd always fit so well together. It's good to see we still do.

But this could be our last time.

I turn toward her. I reach to take the top off the Purple Rain lip gloss. Jae Lyn takes it from me before I can. Her fingernails are sky blue. She still knows that's my favorite color. Her parents couldn't take that memory from us.

Jae Lyn puts a bit of the Purple Rain lip gloss on her lips. And then she kisses me. It's nice and innocent. Like our very first kiss.

But nothing happens. So we wait.

And fall asleep.

When I open my eyes, six zeroes glow red beneath Jae Lyn's left clavicle. Her eyes are closed. She's still. Quiet. Cool. Stiff.

Shit.

I shake her. She doesn't move.

"Jae Lyn?"

Nothing.

"Jae Lyn!"

Silence.

Funny how things work out the way they do. Karma is a bitch, sometimes.

But hope is a sweet expectation, even if everything happens for a reason.

I kiss Jae Lyn behind her ear, in the spot that used to make her pull me closer, before I lay my head on her chest. Listening for I don't know what. We stay this way long past the start and end of prom.

And then, well after my tears have dried, I feel her fingertips at the small of my back. Stroking. Hesitant. Exploratory.

I shiver. My heart knocks. My hips flatten against the bed.

She remembers.

I don't look at her clock. I don't look at my clock. I just hold her tight.

Gynoid, Preserved

"**I** missed my crowd-funding goal."

Mama's tears fall on my shoulder. My heart-engine sputters. My bio-clock chimes.

Twenty-four hours left.

0 0 0

Daddy had been clear when I brought Jean-Loup home for dinner the first time:

"If you take my daughter to Chicago, I cut off your balls. If my daughter goes to visit you in Chicago, I cut off your balls."

Daddy is a neurosurgeon. New money. Northbrook bougie. He gets off on sharp instruments.

Mama had also been clear when I brought Jean-Loup home for dinner the first time:

"If you go visit him in Roseland, you will not come home. The Haitian gangs will kidnap you and beat you and rape you and ransom you and hook you on drugs, and then kill you."

She'd said this at the dinner table, with Jean-Loup sitting right next to me.

Mama is a heart surgeon. Old money, Chicago South Side bougie. Lab School educated.

She knew better.

She'd learned in first grade that Jean-Baptiste Point du Sable founded Chicago as a center of trade and industry. She'd learned he'd been a handsome, charming man. She'd learned his shrewd trading skills and badass charisma got him elected Chicago's first mayor. She'd learned he molded Chicago into a formidable city-state during his six terms in office.

She knew better.

She'd been taught at the knee that her great-great grandfather, Etienne Jean-Louis, helped make Chicago a world-class city with iron ore and railroads. She'd passed his iron and steel mills every day on the way to school, watching from the back seat of her mama's Bentley as trains approached on tracks he owned.

So for Mama to reduce my boyfriend's city (her hometown!) to a gang war between the Ro Boys in Roseland and the Wash Boys in Washington Heights—because bougie-ass Fernwood, where she grew up, was caught in the middle—

Well, she knew better.

0 0 0

I told Mama her crowd-funding campaign wouldn't work.

Money wasn't the issue. Her bougie suburban friends in Northbrook and Highland Park and Kenilworth have gobs of it. They were just tired of hearing her brag.

For two years, they listened to Mama go on about Blanford Sutton's 3D printers (they can render an epidermis, dermis, and hypodermis with ninety-nine percent accuracy); my soft skin (all-natural collagen); my beautiful, textured, springy curls (each individual hair grows out of my dermis with a cortex and multiple layers); and my artificial hemoglobin (designed to sustain the collagen in my skin and the keratin in my hair).

Mama should've done it the other way first: crowd-fund my first year, and then drop her and Daddy's money into my second and third year. That way, she could brag about me having Blanford Sutton's Black Platinum Package (all of my memories intact, as far back as eighteen months old), and she and Daddy would still have some money left over to be the Joneses of Northbrook. Blanford Sutton's referral discount is deep.

With this strategy, six months into my commissioning, three of Mama's friends would have been knocking on the door, asking for her referral code. Two had junkie kids caught up in the never-ending opioid avalanche who OD'd three weeks apart, and another had a gasper who liked to be choked while being tickled. Those three referrals would have put me through my second year of university.

Now, my only hope is tweezer-clumsy hasbros.

0 0 0

Mama tries to put on a bright smile, more for her than for me. "Don't worry. We still have Plan B. Cermak Road kardia work fast. Remember their motto: 'Give us one hour, and we'll give you another year.'"

I sit on the couch. "You said they were a rip-off. Con artists. Failed heart surgeons and wanna-be roboticists."

Twenty-three hours and forty-seven seconds.

Mama pulls a tissue out of her sleeve and dabs at her eyes. "Now I'm saying, I can't fix you, and they're all you have right now."

Twenty-three hours and thirty-two seconds.

"I don't want to go. I just want to spend my last hours here, with you and Daddy."

Twenty-three hours and twenty-six seconds.

Mama tries to pull me up. "If we leave now, we can be in Chicago in less than an hour."

Twenty-three hours and seventeen seconds.

"They may need to order parts for my heart-engine. That can take days. Weeks, even."

Twenty-three hours and twelve seconds.

Mama pulls harder. "Trust the motto."

Twenty-three hours and seven seconds.

I don't budge. My tears are sudden. "Blanford Sutton Industries called earlier. My pickup is tomorrow at 3 p.m. They'll provide the box."

As usual, the internet is right. I don't have a self-preservation program.

0 0 0

I met Jean-Loup my junior year at the annual Rock Island co-ed track and field invitational. He was a hurdler, too, 300 metres, just like me.

He tried to give me some tips on my form before the prelims. He'd said, "Gen bèl fòm. But you need to strengthen your trail leg hip flexor."

He was showing off under lights, in front of the crowd. His chest flexed often under his Chicago Leo singlet.

Out there, in Rock Island, they go completely ape-shit bananas for track meets. They pack the stadium on Friday nights for the fleet-footed crimson and gold Rocks like they do for football and them good ol' boys down in Texas.

"That lovely knee of yours don't need no scar."

I couldn't get enough of his Haitian Creole and his accent. But I played it cool.

I told him, "The last time my trail leg, or my lead leg, hit a hurdle was last year. Forty-four races ago. I placed second in state that day—as a sophomore."

And then I psych-tivated my Auricle, willed Janelle Monáe's "Electric Lady" as loud as I could stand it, and high back-kicked with excellent form for a warm-up lap around the track.

I didn't look back.

0 0 0

Every night, for the past three nights, Mama, Daddy, and I have lain in bed, in the dark, waiting for the arrival of my six zeroes.

Mama watches the digital red numbers on my chest, just beneath my skin, count down. I watch the red glow from my bio-clock illuminate the tears on Mama's cheeks and the snot on her upper lip.

Daddy snores.

When morning comes, Daddy goes into the bathroom and sobs. All day.

Every so often, words, broken and torn, are wrenched from his throat. His lament is clear: Blanford Sutton Industries is an evil corporation; my lack of a self-preservation program is by design to force bereft parents to re-commission their beloved, twice-grieved daughters as a gynoid another year.

When night falls, we all climb back into bed. Mama resumes her watch. Daddy snores, spent of emotion. And I watch Mama, wondering if my love of life has truly left me.

0 0 0

I died in Jean-Loup's bed.

His sheets smelled of boy. I love the smell of boy.

Jean-Loup had been stroking my left eyebrow with his thumb when I was shot in the head.

"Mwen renmen sousi w," he'd said.

He loved my thick and heavy dark brows. He loved how they felt after I got them threaded. He loved how they framed the beauty of my face.

He wasn't trying to be cool or suave or smooth brown brother about it. He wasn't trying to show off.

He just loved me.

This is my last memory as a real girl, my anchor memory, untouched by the bullet that ripped through his bedroom wall and into my brain.

0 0 0

Some gynoid named Jae Lyn in Highland Park (the next town over) posted a holo-vid about re-upping for the first time.

She said, despite the smiley roboticists in your face telling you the paralysis is only temporary, and despite the piles of fleece blankets the nurses tuck under your chin because Blanford Sutton's lab suites are cold as hell, if you establish a nice, happy anchor memory before your bio-clock winds down (and you must do this as close to six zeroes as possible), that anchor memory will settle your mind when you wake up, you won't go batshit crazy when your limbic system struggles to kick in, and you'll feel all warm and tingly once it does because that anchor memory will jumpstart your self-preservation behaviors and it will be the very first memory you recall on the other side.

The loveliest memory ever retrieved.

So, as I lie here on the couch, Mama strokes my brow, my bio-clock ticks down its final seconds—*nine, eight, seven*—I close my eyes—*six*— latch onto the memory of Jean-Loup leaning over me—*five*—hear him whisper, "Mwen renmen sousi w"—*four*—(I love your eyebrows)— *three*—my heart-engine begins its shut down—*two*—everything goes quiet—*one*—

And I smile.

In the Marrow

Welcome to Obvix, Zakiya. What would you like me to do for you today?
Check my holo-messages.

Checking your holo-messages now. Retrieved one holo-message for you.
Play.

Before I play this message, Zakiya, I should warn you: It is from Gynoid Number 98963221. She has been registered with the Institute for Sexually Deviant Robots. She has also been placed on the do-not-answer list by your mother.

Was my mother home when she called?

Yes, but as you — *static* — persuaded me to do, I squelched the ring tone before it hit the house circuits and then sent the call straight to your holo-mail.

Hacked, Zee Dub. I hacked you. It's a real word. You can say it.

...

Fine. Play message, please.

Saturday, June 28
12:47:06 p.m.
Transmission downloaded.
Transmission placed in queue.
Transmission will begin in 3, 2, 1 —

I know I'm the last person you want to see right now. So I'll make this quick. I'm not your Jae Lyn de la Rosa. But you probably already know that.

[She looks down]

I'm sorry I didn't kiss you back. I'm sorry I pushed you away. I'm sorry I haven't returned your calls. I'm sorry my Jean Grey impression sucked.

Or maybe it didn't. Depends on which resurrection we're talking about.

I could blame my parents. They deleted all of your messages. Not like they really wanted us to be together in the first place. But I'm sure that doesn't make you feel any better.

I could also blame my programming. But I think pushing you away was all me. The me deep down in here somewhere trying to figure out what the hell is going on.

I know that doesn't make you feel any better. But it doesn't make me feel any better, either.

[Heavy sigh]

The more I think about you, the more I think about that kiss.

[Looks up with slow, adorable shy smile]

That was a damn good smooch, girl. I could feel all your sexy.

[Long pause]

It just surprised me.

[Smile is now gone]

Look, I don't know you. You say you were my girl before I died, but I don't remember you. Maybe it was the brain cancer. Maybe it messed up my memory. My parents say they paid Blanford Sutton's coders a crap-ton of money to extract my memories and keep them intact. Every single one of them.

[Quick, adorable, fierce scowl]

Which is total bullshit. I mean, when I think of you, when I think of us, I get —

[Closes eyes]

Nothing. Except for that kiss.

[Opens eyes shimmering with tears]

You seem like a nice girl. I want to know you. I want to remember you. In my marrow. That's why I'm making a fool of myself now, right? This is really embarrassing, by the way.

[Wipes tears away]

Whatever. I'm just going to say it. You're a red-blooded American girl. I have a red artificial hemoglobin blood surrogate. It even says so on my manufacturer's certificate.

[Adorable shy smile again]

By the way, that's a deviant gaybot girl pick-up line. So... Call me.

I just texted you the new number. I bought it on BlackBook, because fuck the ISDR and fuck my parents.

I want to know what I was like. What we were like.

I want to know you. Again.

Transmission ended.

Little Miss Saigon

Now:

I wake with a start and fall out of my chair. My entire body is sleep-stiff. I can't feel my legs. It's a struggle to crawl into bed.

The sheets are cool, even though the broken hotel air conditioner sputters its last breaths to keep out the humid Ho Chi Minh morning. Rehani is gone. She took Isabella.

My clothes are strewn all about the room. I think Rehani did that to slow me down. Funny that. I couldn't be more lethargic right now if I were asleep.

It takes some time for the circulation to return to my legs before I can get out of bed. As soon as I'm able, I pull on my clothes as fast as my still-sluggish body will allow: black-and-white Billionaire Boys Club ringer T-shirt; super-baggy khaki Regatta shorts; red, white, and black Ferrari Speed Cat Super Lite Pumas. Had I known we were going to Vietnam when I woke up yesterday morning, I would have dressed a little less high-end street and a little more bou'gie bleek.

Rehani didn't take the backpack. Our passports are still there. So is Isabella's manufacturer's certificate of origin. That doesn't comfort me, though. Just because Rehani didn't leave the country doesn't mean she and Isabella won't be hard to track within the myriad of unfamiliar scents that smell nothing like her.

I shoulder the backpack, close the door behind me, and limp to the elevator bank on still-wobbly legs. In the lobby, the young girl at the front desk greets me good morning, her white áo dài sheer beneath the split at her hip. I ignore her.

I can't smell Rehani. Or Isabella. I'm not sure if I even know what this Isabella smells like. We've had her less than a day.

But I flare my nostrils anyway and push open the hotel entrance double doors leading out to Nguyễn Văn Cừ. Still nothing. I refuse to panic.

There's a mall to the south. I'm certain Rehani didn't go that way, even if I can't smell for shit. Her hunger, her instincts—just like mine—would drive her into the countryside or to sparse, secluded areas of Ho Chi Minh City. Those would be the best places to eat our daughter, uninterrupted.

So I set off in the opposite direction.

0 0 0

Two days ago:

Cora Juniper Jackson put a Rickard's Red in front of me on the marble kitchen island and asked: "What's your favorite memory of Isabella?"

I couldn't help but smile. "That's an easy one: taking a daily nap with her. She would put her head on my chest and fall asleep the moment we laid down. Without a whimper. Without a cry. And she would stay that way for as long as I slept." I took a sip of my Rickard's. "She was such a good baby."

"But even now, you're still grieving for her."

I nodded because my voice would break if I spoke.

Some routine this interview was turning out to be.

Not that I believed Cora when she promised me and Rehani that last week. I'd done my research. I'd blackjacked her. The Dictionary Man told me all her business.

Cora had been one of the youngest United States Mensa members at three years and two months. She did Alicia Keys covers and impersonations—piano and all—on the weekend, which was why she wore a fedora and a white ribbed tank top now. Five hours before, she'd played a gig at the Soul Spot in Chicago before flying into Toronto on a Blanford Sutton Industries private jet.

This condo was her neutral site, where she conducted all her final interviews with mothers and fathers wanting Blanford Sutton daughters. She did them here to put the parents at ease, and to make them nervous as hell.

People like Cora didn't do routine. People like her had lives that were anything but routine.

Cora rinsed some asparagus in a colander at the sink before breaking off the white bottoms. "And what's your worst memory of Isabella?"

That one was easy, too.

0 0 0

Now:

My stomach rumbles as I make my way up Hai Bà Trưng. I step fast around clusters of toothless old women selling fruits and vegetables, strong young men unloading crates of beer from small trucks onto the sidewalk, and the occasional scantily clad bargirl standing outside darkened doorways that beckon with the clink of glasses.

I don't know where I'm going. Everything smells like Rehani. Nothing smells like Rehani. When I pause to get my bearings, desperate to pick up her scent, six little brown children swarm me.

"Hello!" they say. "Hello! Hello! Hello!"

All six children are shirtless, and only one has footwear. Filthy, over-sized pink flip-flops are clasped between her filthier toes.

The children shove sticks of Wrigley's spearmint gum into my just-as-brown hands. "Buy! Buy! Buy!" they say. I give them the handful of American quarters in my pocket.

I smile as they run down the street looking for the next foreign face. It's nice, for once, to feel this hunger again. I don't mind this hunger. I trust this hunger. I know this hunger won't drive me to chase down those children, snatch them up, tear off hunks of their supple flesh, and gorge on their bloody goodness.

But I also know that other hunger, the dark hunger, will soon win out. I just hope that time hasn't come for Rehani yet.

0 0 0

Two days ago:

"We'd been playing with Isabella on the beach in Khao Lak when the tsunami hit Thailand eight years ago. It had been her first time on sand.

"Isabella wouldn't put her feet down. Not after that first hesitant touch of warm sand on those smooth pink soles of hers. Each time Rehani or I went to set her down, Isabella would lift her chubby little legs and just hold them there. It looked as if she was sitting in midair. I guess she just didn't like the texture of sand.

"Rehani noticed the water first. With the light and the distance, it looked like a solid bank of very low white clouds rolling in from the horizon. It was such an odd sight, especially when you consider the sky was mostly blue with high, wispy, white clouds.

"We didn't realize the tsunami for what it was until it swept over a fishing boat. Just swallowed it whole. That's when the people at the edge of the water started pointing and shouting. That's when we should have run.

"But the water was so mesmerizing. Fascinating. As it bore down on us—stretching across the entire horizon—violent, white sprays burst up to the sky, as if the water was angry at us. Or showing off. Or both.

"That's when people started running. Rehani snatched up Isabella, and I scooped up our backpack. I left the towels, books, and sunscreen. We didn't look back. We didn't have to. We already knew it was too late.

"I'd never seen Rehani cry until then. She sobbed my name. That was the only word she spoke as she ran. Isabella was clutched tight to her chest, but Rehani never broke stride.

"I didn't say anything. I just ran, two steps behind Rehani and Isabella, hoping that solid mass of water would hit me first. Hoping I could shield and protect my two beautiful girls.

"I should have known better. It hit me hard. I was surprised by its force. We'd just made it to the other side of the beachfront bungalows. It knocked me right off my feet, slammed me into Rehani and Isabella, and then skewered me onto some splintered wood.

"And as if that wasn't shitty enough, it swept both my girls away from me. All I could do was scream their names until I couldn't scream anymore."

0 0 0

Now:

I cross the crazy-busy street, just like how the Ho Chi Minh Lonely

Planet tells me: slow and steady, into the endless wave of motor scooters so they can see me and avoid me. Halfway to the other side, I stumble and nearly fall.

I've picked up Rehani's scent.

Tinny-sounding scooter horns beep with adorable anger all around me. I ignore them as I keep moving. Faster now.

Her scent is faint. Sickly sweet. Much like a mango left out too long.

Yeah, I know; there are probably scores of mangoes like that for sale within a six-block radius of me. But I also know this is Rehani's scent.

She's going ripe fast. It won't be long before the hunger takes her completely.

Shit.

0 0 0

Two days ago:

Cora pulled a wooden cutting board and a knife from the storage space inside the kitchen island and brought me two yellow onions from the walk-in pantry. "Tell me about the healing process."

My Rickard's Red paused at my lips. I wasn't quite sure what she meant or where she was going with this. Did she mean me? Did she mean Rehani? Did she mean our psychological and emotional healing after we lost Isabella?

The last thing I wanted to do was fuck this up. Rehani deserved to have Isabella back. Besides, she'd drop my ass like a bad habit if I messed up this daughter-buy.

I could hear Rehani playing with this Isabella upstairs in the lofted space of the once bell tower church. This Isabella laughed exactly like our Isabella did.

Cora put the asparagus into a roiling saucepan on the stove, reduced the heat somewhat, and then added a few spoonsful of bacon fat into the skillet.

"It's not a trick question," she said, cutting the asparagus stalks in half and then slicing them at a diagonal. "Debris turned you into shashlik—a shish kabab. How did you heal?"

I must have looked like a man who'd just heard he wouldn't be granted a reprieve at the eleventh hour, because when Cora looked up from the asparagus, she laughed her ass off.

"Wash your hands, chop those onions as thin as you can, and then tell me what it's like to be one of the living dead."

0 0 0

This is what I mostly left out of my interview with Cora two days ago, but she found out anyway through the Dictionary Man:

I'm a delta child. So is Rehani. Twenty-six years ago, our moms and fifty-eight other pregnant women wanted perfect, beautiful babies. So they took drugs.

Good thing that turned out so well.

Our moms had been part of an experimental prenatal drug research program at Great Lakes Naval Hospital in Chicago. The researchers had enticed all sixty knocked-up women with the promise of super-healthy children for the first twelve months of our fragile little lives.

The researchers also promised the first-time mothers—the only qualifier for the experiment—an assload of money, in case a healthy child wasn't enough of an incentive.

Two months into the program, twenty women miscarried. The researchers labeled those dead fetuses "alpha children."

Three months into the program, twenty women bore their children premature. The researchers labeled those eager beavers "beta children."

Nine months into the program, my moms, Rehani's moms, and the eighteen remaining women had uneventful births. The researchers labeled us "gamma children." The normal ones.

That is, until we turned sixteen, and half of us started to rot from the inside. Then the researchers called us "delta children."

We didn't heal. Not even the smallest cut. Our skin sloughed off. Our blood turned thick and viscous and black. It stank like nobody's business.

I would wake up in the middle of the night, my sheets soaked through with awful chunks of decayed me. I thought I was disintegrating. It hurt like hell.

It was worse for Rehani.

As a boy, I could get away with smelling like that. At least, in the beginning when the smell wasn't so bad. But for Rehani and the other four delta girls, the decaying process was accelerated.

The researchers thought it had something to do with their period and the shedding of their uterine lining. They thought all those "womanly things" going on down there somehow made the girls decay faster and smell worse than the boys.

I'd call bullshit on that wonderful theory, but I don't know nothin' 'bout birthin' no babies. Or what to do when Aunt Flo decides it's go time.

Anyway, we were such the enigma and fascination to our researchers. We were special. They adored us so much, they locked us away. All ten of us. They wanted us all to themselves.

To this day, I don't know where they put us. I just know it was the cliché of every science fiction movie: cold and bright with white floors and white walls. Not that it matters where they held us. The place is empty now. No one's there.

We ate them all. Guards. Researchers. Assistants. Even the pompous government administrators.

They tasted the best.

0 0 0

Two days ago:

"What did they taste like?" Cora transferred the onions from the skillet onto a porcelain dish.

"Lunch." I was proud of myself for pulling that one off with a straight face.

"So"—she began, as she placed the six liver slices she'd asked me to season with salt, pepper, paprika, and dry mustard into the skillet—"if you ate me after dinner tonight, I'd taste like this."

It wasn't a question. I felt saliva squirts at the back of my jaw as the meat began to fry.

"Good thing I seasoned those to my liking," I said, also proud my straight face didn't falter.

"Would I even satiate you?"

I looked Cora up and down. "An appetizer, at best."

Cora lifted her chin at the simmering asparagus on the stove. "Drain that, put it in the bowl on the counter, and then tell me why you aren't a rotted, putrescent mess right now, dripping all over my kitchen."

0 0 0

Looking back at that moment two days ago:

I'd bet a whole pan of my moms' peach cobbler that Cora made me season the liver because she'd thought it would trigger my dark hunger.

It definitely explains why her muscle, Ruck, had been standing off to the side with a gun in one hand and another in a shoulder holster.

But the dark hunger doesn't work that way.

Not that I understand it. I just know raw meat doesn't get me slobbering for human flesh.

0 0 0

More of what I mostly left out of my interview with Cora two days ago, but she deduced with that big brain of hers, anyway:

An average-sized, full-grown adult gives me and Rehani a few weeks of total healing and pristine health. The rot is reversed. Skin and organs regenerate. Wounds and broken bones mend within hours. Hair grows back in thick and lush. We smell like newborn babes.

For two years, we fed in remote, off-the-beaten-track locales. The places where a few disappeared people wouldn't even rate a footnote in a newsfeed. Yeah, I know it was shitty. I also know I didn't ask for this.

We backpacked all around Southeast Asia. Thailand. Cambodia. Vietnam. We even did Sumatra for a few weeks.

And then, during our second stint in Thailand, I knocked up Rehani in this secluded Phuket beach bungalow just steps from that blue-within-blue water. She knew it right away. We'd become in tune with our bodies at the cellular level.

That new awareness we now had—sight, smell, taste, touch—scared the hell out of us. Especially when we couldn't bear the dark hunger any longer.

Sometimes, it felt like we were walking around with big Zs tattooed on our foreheads. We just wanted to blend into the background. Become faceless.

But that no longer was an option. We had to step back onto the grid.

We knew people would notice the big, bald Black dude and the tall, stunning Persian-African-Indian girl with the newborn strapped to her chest, browsing bolts of silk and woven handbags at Night Bazaar in Chiang Mai or buying fish and rice at Psah Chas in Siem Reap. And we were cool with that. As long as they didn't notice us eating people.

We put diapers in those woven handbags and we made baby slings out of that silk. We might not have liked what we'd become, but that didn't make us love that Isabella any less.

But always, in the back of our minds, was the urban legend that floated around those bright, white holding cells the Feds had put us in. Devour a baby whole before its tenth month, and we would have total healing for an entire year. No smell. No decay.

Not that either of us really wanted to find out if it were true. But the thought was there. Every day. Niggling. Whispering. Tempting. Seducing.

That's what the dark hunger did to you. It messed with your mind.

It fucked you up good.

0 0 0

Looking back at why I woke up so stiff this morning and how little time I've spent with this Isabella:

When we made the exchange last night at Hotel Nikko Saigon—backpack full of money from me to Ruck; Isabella from Cora to Rehani's loving arms—Rehani couldn't get enough of Isabella.

She nuzzled her neck, taking in Isabella's scent long after Cora and her muscle had left.

Rehani stayed that way the entire night on the hotel bed. Just her and Isabella. I slept in a chair.

That's why I don't know this Isabella's scent.

And no, I'm not jealous. Or bitter. I didn't carry Isabella for nine months. I didn't form that special bond a mother has with her unborn child.

But I for damn sure made Rehani promise not to ever take this Isabella anywhere without me.

0 0 0

Two days ago:

Cora tossed the asparagus in a large bowl with extra-virgin olive oil, lemon zest, Parmesan cheese, and a pinch of salt and pepper. "I'd figured that's why you googled the Blanford Sutton process."

Her words hung in the air for a long moment before silence filled the space. Neither of us spoke. I didn't look at her.

And then, from upstairs, Isabella giggled, long and lovely. Rehani answered with a pure, joyful laugh I hadn't heard in a very long time.

"The Dictionary Man goes both ways, you know," Cora said.

I tried to play it off. "Excuse me?"

She turned the liver over to brown the other side. "The last thing you want to do right now, Clive, is play dumb with me."

I gulped my Rickard's to cover my nervousness.

"Look," Cora said, "I want you to be truthful with me. You need to be truthful with me, if you want any chance of getting a Blanford Sutton daughter. It's what we value. We like candor. Honesty. Veracity."

Cora got three white, over-sized dishes from the cupboard over the sink.

"That's how Blanford Sutton Industries chooses its clients," she continued. "You can have all the money in the world and then some, but if we doubt your integrity, then you don't get one of our daughters."

0 0 0

Why I tried to play off googling the Blanford Sutton process in my interview with Cora two days ago:

Damn right we googled the Blanford Sutton process. Rehani and I had to know if Blanford Sutton daughters were actually eighty-seven percent keratin and collagen.

We'd heard they have an epidermis, dermis, and hypodermis. Google said their hair grows out of their dermis and it has a cortex and multiple layers, just like ours.

Google also said their skin and hair are sustained by a blood surrogate, an artificial hemoglobin that's the best on the market today. Details like that were important to us. Especially Rehani.

We had to make sense of it all. We had to dispel the rumor, once and for all. Or give it life.

Cora had told us all they needed were Isabella's stem cells. The roboticists and genegineers would use them to seed Isabella's synth keratin and synth collagen before attaching both to her mechanical structure.

That sounded real enough to us. Real enough to hug, at least.

Why wouldn't we google that?

We just wanted our daughter back. I just wanted Rehani to be happy again.

0 0 0

The moment during the interview two days ago with Cora when it turned into an inquisition:

"But you and Rehani asked for Isabella to be age-progressed to nine months old." Cora turned the heat off the liver and placed the meat on the cutting board to rest. "That's three months older than she was when she died."

"We just wanted our baby girl back." My voice was almost too soft for even me to hear.

Cora nodded, quiet for a moment. Then she asked: "Who did you want to find first? And don't lie, because I'll know."

0 0 0

Now:

I try not to run.

I keep my strides long and my steps quick. It's a monumental battle of will not to sprint down the sidewalk and knock everybody out the fucking way.

But I'll be damned if Rehani sees me bust through the door like a crazy person, my eyes wild and my chest heaving—even if she did break the one and only promise we'd ever made to each other.

And yeah, I know exactly where Rehani is now. Her scent beckons. It's unmistakable. Heavy. Cloying. Dangerous.

She'll be looking to feed, desperate to stave off the change. If she doesn't feed soon, she won't have the element of surprise.

People will smell her coming from a mile away. Stalking will be difficult. She'll have trouble walking, let alone running. Her muscles and ligaments will quickly deteriorate and shred into ragged fibers. Her femur and tibia will shatter.

I hope she's not at that point yet. I pray she's not at that point yet. But I run, anyway.

0 0 0

This is what naked honesty looked like during the interview with Cora two days ago:

"It took me six days to find Rehani after the tsunami. She'd been at one of those notice boards with information on missing people, looking for her picture. Looking for Isabella.

"I love Rehani, but to be completely honest, I was looking for Isabella.

"I knew Rehani would be fine. I knew that from experience. One cover-of-darkness feeding, and four hours later the hole in my chest from the palm tree branch was gone. So I didn't lose sleep over her.

"But I tossed and turned all five nights thinking about Rehani eating Isabella. And it didn't help at all that Isabella wasn't with Rehani when I found her.

"She couldn't tell me what had happened to our daughter. She'd said she didn't know where Isabella was. Rehani just wept and clung to me and wouldn't let go.

"I wanted to comfort her, but I couldn't. Not at first. Not without knowing Isabella's fate.

"As Rehani sobbed and snotted all over the front of my shirt, I couldn't help but keep thinking over and over:
Thisisbullshitthisisbullshitthisisbullshit.

"I know that sounds harsh. But you don't know the dark hunger. It's brutal. It's powerful. It's unyielding."

0 0 0

This is what naked emotion looked like during the interview with Cora two days ago:

Cora put a bottle of Jackson-Triggs white merlot on ice in a bucket. "You still don't believe her."

Again, it wasn't a question. I sighed, hard and heavy, and rubbed my smooth, bald head.

"I didn't see her ripen and decay once over those next three months." My voice was a bit louder, but just barely. "Rehani claimed her beautiful glow was from the nice, juicy bodies she found in overturned fishing boats and under piles of cars on the remote parts of the beach." Two tears came fast, as if they were racing each other down to my chin. "That was a bad time for us."

Cora handed me another frosty cold Rickard's Red. I nodded my thanks.

"It was wrong of me to accuse Rehani of lies and bullshit as we looked for Isabella all over Khao Lak and Bang La On and Phuket," I went on, taking a long drink of my beer. "Even then, she swore up and down that she'd been feeding on drowned bodies the whole time without me. Maybe she had. I hardly saw her at night."

Cora put a CorningWare dish of wild rice soaked with a cup of water into the microwave and set it for fourteen minutes. "But yet, you lashed out at her."

"Which was stupid. I needed her." More tears join the race. "No one understands me like she does. No one wants me like she does. No one loves me like she does."

"You say she loves you, but those were some serious accusations you threw at her. How do you really know she still does?"

0 0 0

Now:

I don't go in through the front door of the convenience store. Neither did Rehani. That's not good.

I want to believe that everything is Kool & the Gang. I want to believe that Rehani still had the presence of mind not to bust through the front door because she could smell easy pickings in the back.

I don't want to think about Rehani holding Isabella the moment she's overcome with her dark hunger.

But the unmistakable scent of fresh blood isn't comforting.

I won't lie; I wonder if surrogate blood smells like real blood. I wonder if nine months of carrying our Isabella wins out over ten years of dark hunger and this Isabella.

I mean, all we are is collagen and keratin, flesh and blood.

0 0 0

This is what growing doubt and anxiety looked like during the interview with Cora two days ago:

I frowned. "Did Rehani tell you something different during her interview?"

Cora sat down on a stool across from me at the kitchen island. "Think about it. You accused the mother of your only child of eating that very child. I wouldn't be surprised if there was some love lost there."

I raised my left hand and wiggled my ring finger, showing off the simple white gold wedding band Rehani bought me in Japan, where we got married seven years ago. "She put a ring on it, didn't she?"

"Just because she needs you, doesn't mean she loves you."

0 0 0

This has been every day of my life since I turned sixteen years old:

That hunger—the dark hunger—doesn't just sneak up on you. It hits you hard. It hits you fast.

Like that tsunami.

It's impossible to resist. One moment, you're sitting there minding your own business. And the next moment, you're tearing into somebody's hips and thighs.

At least, I do.

That's where all the tasty fatty meat is.

0 0 0

This is what drunken anger and confusion looked like during the interview with Cora two days ago:

"Fuck you." Both my stool and beer were on the floor. I don't remember knocking them over.

Ruck stepped forward like he was about to kick my ass. For a brief moment, I didn't know what the hell was going on. I'd just had a few too many. I wasn't trying to get angry and break shit. Cora and Ruck would know without a shadow of a doubt if I was. An Ikea stool and a beer bottle wouldn't be the extent of it.

Cora raised a hand and Ruck stopped in his tracks like the good dog he was. "Look," she said, "I'm just trying to accurately assess the emotions you and Rehani have for each other. Both the good ones and the bad ones."

"Bullshit." I put the chair back upright and almost missed it when I sat back down. "You're just trying to sabotage the interview."

"Why would I do that? It's already apparent that Isabella loves you two to pieces."

0 0 0

Now:

I don't hear anything but my own breathing as I climb through the broken window and drop into the storage room at the back of the convenience store. The smell of blood is stronger here.

It doesn't take me long to see why. A young girl, maybe fourteen years old and wearing a blue uniform, is sprawled in the corner. Her throat is torn out.

I find another girl in a blue uniform just outside the door in the darkened hallway. A stout boy, also in uniform, is facedown in a room full of dry goods. Both had been quick throat snacks as well.

That's when I start to get anxious.

0 0 0

These were the random thoughts running through my head at some point during the interview with Cora two days ago:

If Cora doesn't give us Isabella, Rehani will kill me. Literally. She'll wait for me to get all nice and juicy and healthy from a recent feed, and then eat me in my sleep.

Balls and all.

Blanford Sutton daughters are expensive as hell. Exclusive.

We've sacrificed so much to get this far.

We paid through the nose for the 3D print of Isabella that Blanford Sutton Industries engineers made with a DNA capture from her cord-blood stem cells.

We paid an arm and a leg for the accurate memories and personality traits the engineers rendered from holo-vids of Isabella.

And we paid out the ass to get those memory and personality accuracies as close as possible to one hundred percent.

It all better work.

And it better be worth it.

We've given our pound of flesh and then some. No exaggeration.

Today is one of those days I wish we hadn't donated our organs.

I don't feel sorry for the small black market org rings. They might be Mom and Pop, but they're making scratch hand over fist off people's desperation.

Somebody somewhere who really needed it probably cried when they heard they were getting a nice, healthy liver. Or kidney. Or lung. Or pancreas.

And if they didn't cry, then their wife or husband or son or daughter did.

And then that somebody probably cried again when the org couriers opened their pouches and saw that our livers and kidneys and lungs and pancreases had turned into a decayed mess of blood and tissue three hours later.

I can see it all over Rehani's face sometimes. She also wonders if those somebodies died because our organs died.

It's probably wrong to feel this way, but I'm happy as hell those org rings don't have the scratch to send competent muscle after us.

Six long years of duping every small org ring in every corner of the world, but it was worth it.

I'm sure of it.

I will love Isabella. Even if she doesn't have a heart, but a bio-electric battery.

0 0 0

This is what gobsmacked drunk looked like during the interview with Cora two days ago:

"So this is the part of the interview where you piss me off?"

I was talking to Cora, but I looked at Ruck. I wondered if I could hang with him for a few punches, grafted bison muscle and all. As if he knew what I was thinking, he showed me his fat, bratwurst-sized middle finger.

I turned back to Cora. "This is where you fuck me around, play with my emotions, and then tell us we can't have this Isabella—even though you say she loves us like our Isabella did?"

"No," Cora said, plating the asparagus, "this is the part of the interview where it ends and I feed you."

I blinked. "We're done?"

"Unless you have something else to say."

0 0 0

These are the focused thoughts running through my head right now:

Rehani has this thing for salty flesh. She can't get enough of people with sodium-rich diets. And she's a picky eater, on top of that. Her food must have the exact amount of saltiness. It's why she usually goes for the throat first.

She says the carotid artery is the perfect way to taste just how salty someone is. If the first person isn't salty enough, she moves on to the next one. And if that person doesn't light up her taste buds, then she keeps searching until she finds someone who does.

Which makes it easy to find her during her hunger urges. You just follow the trail of bodies with their throats torn out. And that's what's bothering me.

Maybe she didn't find anyone before the dark hunger made her settle on the best available option. Like Isabella.

And every parent who's nibbled their newborn's chubby cheeks knows how delicious they are.

Rehani could always put off her hunger longer than any other delta child, though. She usually fought it with a hoodrat-like scrappiness.

But after a while, like the rest of us poor bastards, Rehani has got to eat sometime.

0 0 0

This is what a poor, drunk bastard looked like two days ago when he was told the best news of his life:

I took the broom, dustpan, and paper towels Ruck held out to me. We stared at each other for a long moment, mean-mugging each other something fierce. He flexed his muscles under his three-quarter-length leather coat.

"No, I think that's about it," I said to Cora.

"Good." She sliced the liver into long strips. "Clean up that mess, and then go tell your family dinner is ready."

I paused mid-sweep. My hearing always seemed to play tricks on me after the sixth or seventh or twelfth beer. "We passed the interview?" I asked her. "Isabella is ours?"

Cora shook her head, but she was smiling. "Not quite. I still have some paperwork to do, but you and Rehani need to be available to fly within the next forty-eight hours. No matter where I tell you to be."

I frowned. "What's with the secrecy?"

"No secrecy." Her smile got even more kind. "I just need to find the lowest-bidding country for a visa bribe. Someone out there will let us sell you an underage gynoid on their soil. But don't worry. You bring the money, and I'll bring your daughter."

0 0 0

Now:

A brassy, meaty scent like nothing I've smelled before draws me from the back office to the public restrooms. The back of my jaw tingles with saliva squirts.

This isn't stomach-rumbling hunger. This is the approach of violence and rage and want.

It begins to flood me. Fill me.

Shit. I don't want to find Isabella like this.

That brassy smell is stronger on the other side of the women's restroom door. I move to push it open, and then stop. The push panel on the door is smeared with a fresh bloody handprint.

I touch my index finger to the blood, and then the blood to my tongue. There's so little of it.

But it tastes so good. I want more.

That's when I hear Isabella scream.

0 0 0

This is what a poor, drunk jealous bastard looked like two days ago:

I kissed my teeth as I slid the shards of broken bottle from the dustpan into the blue recycle bin.

"So," I asked Cora, "did you put Rehani through this much shit and make her work this hard with the appetizer during her interview?"

Cora snickered at me. "Didn't need to. Rehani sharpened right up from the Asian Summers she made with the Grey Goose L'Orange I told you to bring. Her interview took just fifteen minutes, so we spent the rest of her time drinking until we couldn't feel our lips anymore."

I sat back down on my stool, my bottom lip stuck out longer than a four-dollar popsicle, as my moms would say. I wanted to be the one who bonded with Cora. I wanted to be the one who made me and Rehani a family again.

0 0 0

Now:

It doesn't take me long to find Rehani.

She's in a tiny office, feeding on what looks to be an older woman wearing the same blue uniform as the two girls and the boy. Most of the woman is gone.

I haven't seen Rehani eat that much in one sitting since the government facility. I suppose I shouldn't be surprised. Her scent did nearly knock me over once I found it.

I back out of the office, nice and slow. A delta child has yet to attack another delta child while feeding, but that doesn't mean it can't happen. We all smell like food at some point.

Not that I really want to watch Rehani eat. Sometimes, watching another delta child within the throes of the dark hunger can trigger mine—even if we don't all feed the same.

Besides, I still need to find Isabella.

0 0 0

These are the unfocused thoughts running through my head right now:

It was a squeal. Isabella squealed. She didn't scream.

Or maybe she did scream. Maybe it was a scream of laughter. Of pure delight.

This is what happens when the dark hunger hits. Perception becomes distorted. Rationale nonexistent. Senses muddled.

Except for sense of smell and taste.

I don't even know what I heard anymore. At first, it sounded as if Isabella was in the women's restroom, dying. Her blood surrogate bleeding out.

I've heard that sound before. When Rehani was stalking. First, a high-pitched scream. Then choking. Burbling. It's the same sound people make when Rehani rips out their throat. Man or woman.

Or child?

I've seen the blood, as it flows onto the ground with a bit of rhythm. Pumped out by a slowing heartbeat. Until it's all gone.

But it's never all gone. We devour them before it's all gone.

I shake my head. Rehani wouldn't do that. Not to her daughter. But the blood on the door, it says otherwise.

There are probably pieces of my baby girl on the floor. In the women's restroom. Right now.

In the stall. Behind the toilet. Dropped, unnoticed, there because Rehani stuffed her mouth so fast and so full.

She probably perched on the toilet seat. So nobody would see her feet. Tore off hunks of Isabella. Spilled her blood. Gobbled her up quick. Desperate to not have a witness to the only taboo that both fascinates and shames us delta children.

Because she knew I was coming for her.

No. My love wouldn't do that. My heart, my soul, my all, she wouldn't do that.

Rehani, I know you wouldn't—I know you didn't—

0 0 0

These are the focused thoughts running through my head right now, parallel with the unfocused thoughts:

Rehani, I'm so sorry.

I was angry in Thailand. I was stupid. I was hurt. I shouldn't have insinuated otherwise.

I'd thought I lost you—and Isabella—forever. And then, when I saw you, and not her—

That was the worst day of my life.

I lashed out at you. I blamed you. I attacked you. Because I didn't have her. Because we didn't have her.

We were broken. We weren't a family anymore. But I knew you didn't eat our baby girl. I always knew—

0 0 0

This is me, right now, happy, focused and unfocused, hungry and dangerous:

I hear Isabella again. This time, her wonderful voice comes from the front of the store.

I inch forward. I'm in full stalking mode. I peek around the wall.

A young girl in a blue uniform holds Isabella near the cash register. Another girl smiles and coos and chatters in Vietnamese at her. They pass her back and forth. Isabella loves it.

My baby girl grins right back at them. Shows her pink, toothless gums. Flashes her dimples.

The girls nearly swoon from her cuteness. They take turns kissing Isabella's chubby cheeks. They can't get enough of her. My baby girl can't get enough of them.

She basks in their attention. She revels in their adoration.

She extends a small pudgy hand to each girl. She opens and closes it. Each girl places kisses in her palms. With delight. With reverence. As if she's royalty. Or. Some sort of infant-goddess.

She squeals again.

I take a deep breath. Sweat runs down my face. Into my eyes. I try to blink it away.

I don't want Isabella to see me this way. I try to hold off my dark hunger.

Goddamn, this is so hard!

She's my baby girl. She remembers. Everything. That's how Blanford Sutton Industries made her.

And now, this will be her last memory.

Just as I surge forward, someone grabs me. From behind. Rehani. She whirls me around. She kisses me. She still has gore around her mouth.

"I'm so sorry," she says. "I went out to get some moisturizer for Isabella's skin, and then I got hungry."

I lick Rehani's face. I savor the blood. The bits of flesh. All of it.

"Wait here," she whispers.

I push forward. Again. Rehani is stronger. She's just eaten. She throws me halfway down the darkened hall. But she moves fast. Out into the store. To get Isabella.

Rehani knows how it is. Caught up. In the dark hunger. I eat whatever flesh I can. Whatever flesh I can grab.

The real kind. Maybe even the synth kind. Young girl. Baby girl.

I'd like to think I wouldn't. That I can choose. But I don't have that bond with my baby girl.

I didn't carry her for nine months. I didn't fight the tsunami for her. I didn't lose her. Forever.

(I think all of this in the three seconds it takes me to get across the store.)

And now, face-to-face with this Isabella—my Isabella—she gives me that lovely smile of hers.

And I make a choice.

I choose blood.

Panic Twice, Spin

You first noticed the miniature black hole in the corner of the play-room halfway into book one of the *Cyber Sakura Seven* series.

Your little sister, Mahina, was playing *Panic Twice, Spin*. Nintendo's warning about cosmic repercussions was in big, bold red letters on the back of the game case, but you had thought nothing of it when you bought it with your allowance for Mahina's re-up day. It was a game about fighting zombie-ninjas, for goodness' sake. Besides, you used to play it all the time before Mahina died.

You had just gotten to the part of your book where Sakura's cyber-suit is fused to her skin when you heard an odd sound in the corner of the playroom, left of the holo-vision. "That sounds like God flushing His toilet," you thought. "But far, far away."

Mahina, of course, heard nothing. And for good reason.

Three zombie-ninjas had just spewed green-black ichor and lique-fied internal organs at her face, so she had to drop down into a James Brown split, which only got her one hundred points (even though it was a defensive Level Three move) because she wasn't wearing the short, black, pointy holo-boots. You had told Mahina she would have to buy that upgrade pack with her own allowance when you bought *Panic Twice, Spin* for her earlier that day at the game store.

But you weren't being mean when you told her that. In fact, you were being nice, just like your parents had asked you to do before they left. You were being a mature twelve-year-old. You were playing the part of the older sibling well. You only wished your parents were here to see it.

The nanny had told you your father was in Japan for his business and your mother was in China for hers, and they would meet up in

Hawai'i and fly back home on their private jet sometime next week. Which was fine with you. For once, you were enjoying your little sister's company.

You just couldn't get enough of watching her play *Panic Twice, Spin*. There was something so adorable about it. Not like before, when she would play your game all the time and never ask your permission.

The old Mahina had almost been obsessive about that game. Like you, she just couldn't get enough of it. She would sneak and play it all the time before she died. She had completed every storyline and almost every side quest, except the zombie-ninjas under the moon one. And she was doing so well with it now.

Mahina didn't stay in her split for long. She chained it to a windmill: a leg sweep started the move, while her forearms and back took the brunt of the roll on the hardwood floor. Her momentum was continuous and fluid as her skinny little brown legs spun in a lethal V.

Those zombie-ninjas didn't stand a chance.

Mahina took their legs off at the knees. Their rotted stumps went flying, end over end, landing off-screen. She laughed as she rolled and spun.

You couldn't help but smile. This Mahina had the exact same laugh as the old Mahina. Your mother and father had made sure she was programmed that way. It was wonderful to hear again.

When your parents had told you they were going to buy a Blanford Sutton Industries re-up to replace the old Mahina (sparing no expense, including a full memory upgrade to the hour before she was run down in the crosswalk by that drunk driver), you had thought the new Mahina would sound like a robot. It made sense, considering Blanford Sutton Industries called her a paedroid. But this re-up was just like your little sister in every single way—especially when it came to difficult and intricate dance moves.

Mahina knew the last move of a combo chain was crucial for max points, so she ended her attack with a stab: head down; one skinny little arm fully extended and supporting her entire body weight; torso twisted toward the holo-vision; skinny little legs angled overhead—stiff, straight, and bent at the waist.

For five seconds, she held the move. One thousand points. And then, the zombie-ninjas broke her concentration with a barrage of shiny shuriken, thrown with adept accuracy, despite being legless and prone.

It was only instinct that saved Mahina.

Without thinking, she executed a leg sweep again, shifting from her stab into continuous flares, grateful for the gymnastics training your mother had made your nanny drag Mahina to from the day she turned two and a half years old until the day of the hit-and-run accident last year. This time, not one, but two of her skinny little arms alternated in bearing her weight as her skinny little legs flared up and down—stock-straight, with a wide, saddle split—deflecting the six ninja stars right back at the zombie-ninjas.

Mahina smiled at the satisfying *chunk!* sound the shuriken made as they pierced the zombie-ninjas' soft skulls and stuck fast within their rotted brains. Five hundred points each.

But she had no time to celebrate. A new horde of zombie-ninjas materialized from the shadows on all sides of her, moonlight glinting off their katanas.

You looked over at the black hole. God had flushed again, and the cosmic swirl was now larger.

Mahina flowed from her flares into a standing position, placed her feet shoulder-width apart, and snapped a Michael Jackson front kick. The zombie-ninjas hesitated. Three hundred points.

She tilted the brim of her black, cyber-coded fedora down over her eyes. The zombie-ninjas leaned back as one. Five hundred points. She grabbed her crotch. Negative five hundred points. The zombie-ninjas shuffled closer. Mahina frowned.

But it was all good. She'd just remembered one of the defensive combo chains in preparation for melee combat. Mahina crossed her feet at the ankles, twirled—once, twice, three times—and came to a perfect stop, facing the holo-vision and the holo-game console, balanced on her tip-toes. Eight hundred points.

You glanced at the black hole. It was shrinking.

Mahina grinned. She could feel the charisma boost coursing from her fedora through her body and into the game console. So she decided to go for the taunt bonus.

She snatched one of the peripherals from the floor—a cyber-microphone stand—and adjusted it to her height. The zombie-ninjas flung their katanas to the side as one. Mahina grabbed the mic stand with both hands. The zombie-ninjas snapped their heads back in a bring-it-on gesture. Mahina closed her eyes, tilted her head toward the full moon, and swayed a few shimmies of the Axl Rose snake dance. Sonic charge. The zombie-ninjas turned to the side, dangled one arm in front, one arm behind, bent their knees, and thrust their pelvises three times. Sonic charge counter.

Determined to land the first blow, Mahina unleashed her "Welcome to the jungle!" sonic screech anyway, even though their counter diminished its charge to just five seconds. Her sonic screech had little impact.

The zombie-ninjas went on the attack, and, as one, brought their decrepit right feet down with a mighty stomp. Flesh flew. The ground shook. Mahina stumbled. Her voice wavered. Her sonic screech dissipated into the holo-night air above. Her charisma dropped two points.

Relentless, the zombie-ninjas pressed their advantage.

The martial arts monsters formed straight lines, six rows deep. They stood at attention. They raised their arms over their heads and clapped, as one. The sonic blast knocked Mahina off her feet. The mic stand went flying across the playroom and slammed into the wall on the far side. Negative fifteen hundred points. The black hole grew larger. The sound swirled. You frowned.

In unison, the zombie-ninjas lunged left, dragging their right foot across the ground. Seismic charge. The zombie-ninjas stood at attention again and stomped. The ground buckled. Mahina fell. The zombie-ninjas lifted their left shoulders, then their right shoulders. They looked right, and then left. Taunt bonus: five hundred points.

Scowling, Mahina kicked into a windmill again, but this time the zombie-ninjas were wary. They squatted, hands on their thighs, and horse-stance walked ten steps backward, away from her. Mahina chained her windmill into a spinning one-handed handstand. As long as she kept the spin fast and tight, she would be impervious to any attack the zombie-ninjas sent her way.

But even an eight-year-old paedroid could only keep a spinning one-handed handstand going for so long.

As Mahina began to tire and wobble, she chained her spinning one-handed handstand into a one-handed back handspring. Five hundred points. But she wasn't finished.

Planting her feet wide as she landed, Mahina tilted the brim of her black fedora down over her eyes, grabbed her crotch again, pointed skyward, and screamed. The moon began to run down the night sky in a wide river of pure light, right into Mahina's hand, illuminating her from within. Ten thousand points.

The zombie-ninjas tried to flee, but they couldn't shamble away fast enough on their rotted legs. Mahina put her palm toward the now pitch-black holo-sky, and a flash of light exploded outward from her in concentric waves of white brilliance. You shielded your eyes with your *Cyber Sakura Seven* book. The zombie-ninjas poofed into disintegrated dust. Fifty thousand points.

When you pulled your book down from your face, you saw Mahina grinning and holding a small, glowing white cube in her right hand. She placed her left hand over it. Clean white rays of light shone through her fingers, reaching high into the black holo-sky overhead.

She didn't hold the glowing cube for long, though. Slowly, Mahina pulled her hands apart. As she did so, the cube grew larger. When she was satisfied with its size, she walked over to the black hole in the corner and placed the cube on top of it. The sound of God's flushing toilet stopped. Five hundred thousand points. Side quest completed.

And that's when I appeared.

You hadn't noticed me at first. You put down your *Cyber Sakura Seven* book, picked up the holo-gloves, and asked Mahina, "Could you show me that spinning V move? That was cool."

Mahina was more than happy to show you. She would do anything for her big brother, so she nodded and grinned, took off the cyber fedora and the holo-gloves, and handed them to you. Without cut-eye. Without a fight. Without a snarky comment.

You were surprised. You'd thought, "Maybe Mom and Dad had the snark programmed out of her." You would have done so, were Mahina your daughter.

But then I side-tracked you two when I coalesced into this lovely, curvy, hormone-stirring form from a twisting tornado of long, blue, silky hair that reached down from the moonless holo-sky above (because you and your sister didn't notice my big blue face pulsing and glowing on your holo-vision), and Mahina hit me full on with every iota of her fully intact eight-year-old snark:

"Who are you?" she'd asked me, her little hands on her little hips.

I pretended she wasn't looking at me like I'd just blown a big bubble with her last piece of favorite bubble gum without asking if I could have it, put on an almost-but-not-real smile (snark truly is the antithesis of joy), and said, "Congratulations, Mahina! I am the Once in a Blue Moon Fairy. For your very cool dance moves, and your heroic efforts, which saved the world from some of the most reprehensible creatures known to eight-year-old girls everywhere, I will now grant your wish and turn you into a real little girl!"

I counted ten full seconds of awkward, dead silence. And then, Mahina said:

"I didn't wish to be a real little girl. I don't want to be a real little girl."

My almost-but-not-quite-real smile fell off my face fast. "But every paedroid girl wants to be a real little girl," I insisted. I even lifted my blue wand tipped with a sparkly silver star to show your sister how serious I was.

Mahina just wasn't having it.

"Besides," she told me in that insufferable little voice of hers, "my mom and dad are working very hard right now so I can have at least one more re-up year."

You must have seen the confused look on my beautiful blue face.

"Blanford Sutton Industries," you explained, "only commissions dead daughters for one year. Three hundred and sixty-five days exactly. Once the paedroid's bio-electric battery runs down, that's it—unless the parents buy another year for their daughter."

"And re-upping is not cheap," Mahina said.

"But our parents are rich," you said.

"Very rich," Mahina said.

"And they're getting even richer right now over in China and Japan," you said.

"So, I don't need you to become a real girl," Mahina told me, shaking her head, making her short, eighty-seven percent keratin corkscrew curls fly, "because my mommy and daddy will get me five or ten more years of re-up with all of the money they're making."

Your little sister gave me such the sweetest smile I wanted to eat her up. Right then and there. No, really. Just like those zombie-ninjas she had just defeated.

I wanted to bite into her eighty-seven percent collagen cheek and tear the lab-grown flesh from her face with the tiny little pointed teeth I used for unreasonable little girls like her, and do it over and over and over again, until there was nothing left of Mahina but a bloody stain on your playroom floor.

But instead, I looked at you, and said, "Kaemon, talk some sense into your little sister."

That's when Mahina crooked her little finger at me. I came closer, and she beckoned for me to bend down. When I did, Mahina cupped her hands around my ear and stage whispered, "Maybe you should go find one of those paedroids who really need your help."

I straightened up, transformed myself back into my tornado of blue hair, got the heck out of Highland Park, and did just that.

Her name is Tabitha. She's eight years old, too. She died from leukemia. But now she's very happy. And appreciative. Unlike you two, who will never complete this special look-through I'm giving her into *Panic Twice, Spin II*.

That's right. You heard me.

Now who's laughing?

Me.

(You ungrateful imps.)

The Intersectionality of Race, Gender, and Humanity

Or
Bonquita Jackson, Social Justice Warrior

None of us truly want to die. None of us really want to become someone else.

But the re-up manual helps us to cope during that final year. It calms. It soothes. It removes the fear.

Every morning when I wake up, I start my day with the immortal words of James Brown, just as the manual suggests (in the back, on page 254): I'm Black and I'm proud!

I say it loud; I wear it proud.

But not the dashiki. Or the African medallion.

The hair, though? Yeah, that's me.

That's all me.

0 0 0

I duck under the police tape crisscrossing the entrance of the master bedroom and pause. In the middle of an enormous bed lies a body: face and brains spread across the pillows, headboard, and a good portion of the wall; knees reduced to congealed chunky redness cupped within two deep depressions of the mattress.

Shit. That's some serious blunt force trauma.

That's also my maker.

"Nothing like a game of Whac-A-Mole to roll you out of bed and get the blood flowing," Callahan says. He looks up from his handheld. He gives my re-up bod a once-over for the first time. He looks back down at his handheld.

I'm not offended. My curly 'fro is gorgeous.

"Took you long enough," he says, but he's talking about how long it took to get to the vic, not my new look. "Doré's crime scene boys have already shot their loads and left."

"Good. Can't wait to see what they have to say about it." I lift my chin at the bed. "What's the story?"

Callahan shrugs. "You're the re-up. That's why I called you."

I move to the head of the bed, left of Manford Sutton's body, and bend close to examine the splatter pattern on the wall.

Callahan points to Manford Sutton's crotch. "Doré's boys found dried semen and vaginal secretions on that four-incher of his."

I kiss my teeth. "You say that as if you've got nine inches down your leg."

Callahan doesn't miss a beat. "You'll see when Law Guild pulls my number for re-up."

"What I see is bullshit pouring out of your mouth." I push past Callahan and duck under the police tape out into the hallway. "Coming in I saw uniforms in the living room. We got another body?"

"Something like that. Let's take a walk."

0 0 0

I'd been questioning Johnny Fatlip about stealing the Most Sacred Pearl in the World when I was gunned down in Law Guild, of all places, qualifying me for re-up. He'd been throwing me shade about my small tits and flat ass. I threw him shade right back about his toddler hands and small dick.

Next thing I know, his hired muscle, Ruck, walked into the interrogation room. Put a bullet in my head with his nickel-plated nine millimetre. Just like that. Law Guild holo-vid says it took him all of 0.986 seconds.

Callahan didn't move from behind the two-way mirror. Not even when Johnny Fatlip and Ruck strolled out of the building, bodies of our colleagues on the floor, pooling blood onto the clean, white tiles. He couldn't save me—Law Guild wouldn't let him. Law Guild had made a promise to the Black community. Law Guild had to keep its quota of white police officers killed by Black men.

Which pissed Callahan smooth-the-fuck off.

But, as my Re-Up Black Fairy Grandmother would say (and yes, I just made her up), between you, me, and the fence post, I think Callahan wanted me to re-up. I think he wanted to try his coffee black, for once.

0 0 0

I follow Callahan through the foyer of Manford Sutton's Lake Point Tower condo, and we hook a right down a long hallway that ends at an expansive living room. The far wall is a bank of floor-to-ceiling windows. They curve away from us to our left with the building.

I go to one, cup my hands beside my face, and look out into the night. Fifty-seven floors down is a dark, angry Lake Michigan.

Callahan gestures with his handheld, indicating an area where the living room, kitchen, and dining room come together. "Doré created an interactive three-dimensional holo-rendering of this space."

One of those annoying real estate agents would call it a breakfast nook: small, round, pub-style table and lone wooden chair nestled in the exact center of the bend in the wall. Perfect for a bachelor to read the morning news on his handheld.

"This should be interesting," I say.

Callahan takes a modified Amaray case from an inside pocket of his suit jacket and opens it, removing a brain-computer interface device: cylindrical, grey, and just a few centimetres in length. It matches the one in his right temple. He hands it to me.

I push back my lovely 'fro and put the BCID into the cranial port Law Guild gives all its homicide detectives, including re-upped ones like me. It takes only a fraction of a second to reconcile the real-time breakfast nook with a holographic overlay of the nook three hours ago.

"The hell?"

Seated in the now-occupied chair is a girl: naked; slender arms and legs; stiff, awkward posture; heavy grey veil obscuring her face. At the girl's feet is a black, double-faced sledgehammer. One end is covered with gore.

I tap the inside of my wrists, activating holo-gloves, and lift the girl's veil: glassy eyes; perky, upturned nose; black, pixie-bob haircut. My divine 'fro is more fabulous.

Callahan yawns and wipes his face with a hand. "So, who is she?"

"First-gen gynoid designed by Manford Sutton. I'd heard there were a few still around. S-squared fanboys WC3 them 24-7."

It's Callahan's turn to kiss his teeth. "English, please."

"S-squared stands for Sakura Sweet. Her brand name. She's got this cult following. Fanboys scour the internet day and night trying to find something—anything—about where her early versions might be for their auctions. They query us re-ups hard. You should see some of the holo-vid messages I get."

Callahan smirks. "Geek collecting on a whole new level."

I crouch and touch the sledgehammer. My holo-gloves come away wet. "This is cut and dry, Callahan. You don't need my help on this. Sexbot kills creator. News at eleven."

"Don't go live just yet. Let me show you something."

0 0 0

It didn't help race relations that Law Guild went with a gynoid builder to manufacture re-ups. Each female re-up comes with a free pair of red come-fuck-me boots. Each male re-up comes with an assortment of black attachments. Nine inches is the smallest one.

You can imagine the collective side-eye the Black community gave that.

Law Guild could have just kept it classy and signed a contract with Manford Sutton's twin brother, Blanford. He provides grieving parents who lost daughters another chance to hold their little girls. At least, for a year. If parents want to re-up again, they have to siphon the trust fund.

Before I died, Callahan refused to talk about re-upping. Especially in the morning when we strapped on our sidearms and I wondered aloud what shade of young Black woman I'd be when we returned to our guild suite after being gunned down by some punk whose life narrative was set to the beat of N.W.A.'s "Fuck tha Police."

Of course, now that he's accepted his fate, death by quota, Callahan's re-up dick jokes won't stop. I just fake laugh. He doesn't know the difference.

0 0 0

We go back into the master bedroom and I barely notice the flicker as my BCID kicks in. Sprawled at the foot of the bed is another girl: barefoot; knee-length patchwork quilt skirt; thick black hem; gauzy white scoop-necked peasant blouse; long flared sleeves; eyes open and glassy.

She looks like the girl in the breakfast nook and nothing like the girl in the breakfast nook.

I move closer to get a better look. "The uniforms said nothing about a threesome."

"They wouldn't." Callahan glances at my 'fro. "You scare them."

I pat the ever-growing supernova radiating from my scalp. "Really?" Last week, it was half this size.

"You know what they say, don't you?"

"The bigger the 'fro, the more bounce to the ounce?"

"They say you're a Bad Mamma Jamma. They take their BCIDs out when you come around."

I sigh. "This is why we still need the re-up program. One mind at a time."

Callahan activates holo-gloves of his own, my snark ignored. "S-squared eighty-sixed our boy here with no face, but the evidence doesn't add up." He lifts the gynoid's blouse to just above her slight breasts.

"Should I leave you two alone?"

"Or join in the fun. Look."

He presses a thumb against the gynoid's breastbone and then at the base of her neck.

Six zeroes glow red just beneath the skin of her chest and back. "Doré says her bio-electric battery lasts one calendar year. Our girl here wound down April tenth. But here's the kicker: Doré also says Manford Sutton was murdered April fifteenth."

I nod. It's all starting to make sense. "Security holo-vids show no one going in or coming out of the unit, right?"

"Only Manford Sutton, and not for more than a year." Callahan cocks his head toward the door. "What about that other one? Our boys in Forensics couldn't find her bio-clock."

I shake my head. "The gynoid in the breakfast nook is an early prototype. She's empty inside. Nothing more than a mannequin, really. Manford Sutton couldn't get her quite right. Gynoids are based on his dead girlfriend, but the one in the breakfast nook is a bit off. You can see it in her eyes, nose, and cheekbones. My guess is Manford Sutton wasn't happy with her, but he couldn't bring himself to destroy her, either. So he put her in the corner."

Callahan purses his lips. "I don't get it. You say this isn't sexbot murders creator in the master bedroom with sledgehammer, but it sure as hell looks like it to me. Either I'm missing something, or you're the Amazing Kreskin."

"Only at birthday parties and bar mitzvahs." I smile. "You haven't asked the million-dollar question yet."

Callahan pauses for half a second. "How did the girlfriend die?"

"Bingo. Car crash in Japan. Manford Sutton was driving. The girlfriend had been giving him a blowjob at the time."

Callahan nods, finishing the narrative. "He loved her and he couldn't live without her, so he made a tender-hearted tribute to her." He snorts. "Or he blamed himself for her death and he was still horny, so he made a replica sexbot he could fuck whenever he wanted."

I pick out my 'fro with my clenched fist Afro pick. "No, he loved her. But so did Blanford Sutton, Manford Sutton's twin brother and the self-acclaimed best coder in all the Midwest."

"Get the fuck outta here."

"I bullshit you not." I heard that once on the South Side, where all the Black people live. "Doré ran the prints her boys got off the sledgehammer, right?"

Callahan looks at his handheld. "And the prints from both gynoids. All three sets are identical, belonging to a Naeve Spencer."

I nod again and put my Afro pick back into my marvelous 'fro. "She's the girlfriend. And she's been dead five years."

Callahan sighs, his dimples stretched with weariness. He points at Manford Sutton. "So how did the ghost of Naeve Spencer do this?"

"With an Easter egg combo of fructose, lipids, and proteolytic enzymes cooked up by our boy Manford Sutton."

0 0 0

Callahan now only rages against Law Guild's mandatory re-up policy when our arms and legs are entangled in the dark after a long day at work. "It's outdated!" he snarls. "Don't they realize we know Black lives matter now?"

But we don't.

We who had the life of Riley are not envious of the life of Jamaal. But we fear death. We covet the bio-clock.

We put on these shades of coffee and mocha and caramel and dark chocolate skin because we are seduced by the thought of immortality. Not because we want to feel how uncomfortable Von'Tay and Shinequa's shoes are on their mile-long journey.

(By the way, Law Guild assigned me the name Bonquita Jackson. My rich hazelnut skin is flawless. It's eighty-seven percent collagen. It has an epidermis, dermis, and hypodermis. It's sustained by an artificial hemoglobin blood surrogate. My curly 'fro is awesome. It's eighty-seven percent keratin. It has a cortex and multiple layers. It grows out of my dermis like real hair. My nose is delicate. Its nostrils are wide. Callahan tweaks it when I catch him looking at me in a brief moment of lurve. My lips are beautiful. Full. Plump. Juicy. Callahan likes to bite the lower one. I don't mind. It turns me on.)

Callahan knows this. Everyone knows this. And yet, we all pretend otherwise.

0 0 0

I give Callahan a smarmy smile, like the little shit A-plus student at the front of the class. "Sakura Sweet's bio-electric battery unlocked the latent energy within Manford Sutton's man juice, artificially enhanced with his special blend of fructose, lipids, and proteolytic enzymes and powering her beyond her wind-down date. Some girl in Sweden read Maddie Nice's paper on how her Purple Rain lip gloss can rejuvenate gynoids. Manford Sutton must have read it, too, because he bought Purple Rain from Maddie Nice last month for a couple of billion."

Callahan puts his hands in his pockets, goes up on his tip-toes. "So, that means you know about this Easter egg, then?"

I roll my eyes. I see where this is going.

But then Svetlana Sokolov stalks into Manford Sutton's bedroom on Louboutins my size elevens could never hope to smoosh into. She flashes us her badge, as if we're civilians or poo-putt local law enforcement and not detectives, like her.

"I'm taking over this investigation," she says.

Callahan looks her up and down. "Like hell you are."

Sokolov pushes between us and scowls up at Callahan. "Your murderer escaped its evidence locker. We've got a fucking bloodthirsty robot on the loose out there."

"Gynoid," I say.

Sokolov reaches behind her and puts a middle finger in my face. I smack her hand away. She whirls on me.

"Careful," she says. "Haven't you heard the news? Russian lives matter now."

I kiss my teeth. Sokolov smirks. I pat my 'fro. Sokolov teases her mohawk. Hers is short and edgy. Mine is Soul Nebula fabulous.

"I guess you haven't heard," she says. "Prosti-bot's escape hit social media an hour ago. Trending worldwide. People in Montana are stocking up on jumper cables and defibrillators. Law Guild is doing damage control and has changed policy. Re-ups are all Russian now."

"But ... I *was* Russian, before," I say.

"I suppose you'll have to wait until that re-up comes back around, then." Sokolov walks over to Manford Sutton's bed. "Captain says you're both confined to your guild suite until further notice. The uniforms in the foyer will escort you." She turns, pops the collar of her red trench coat. "Now get the fuck out of my crime scene."

0 0 0

Callahan stops me in the hallway. "Fuck this," he says. "We can be a fucked-up Bonnie and Clyde. You can live forever with that Easter egg combo. I heard a fifth-class chemist put it into Purple Rain lip gloss. You can use that until we run out. And when that day comes, we'll find that fifth-class chemist when we need some more. And we'll kidnap that chemist, put a gun to her head, force her to make us a fuckload of lip gloss, and then drop down to Mexico when things get too hot." He kisses each of my eyelids in turn. "I want you to live forever."

I press my lips to his clavicle. "As long as my 'fro stays fabulous."

And then we pull our police-issue Glocks out of our holsters, thumb the safety, and go meet the uniforms in the foyer.

If Wishes Were

Obfuscation Codes

"Tell the truth and shame the devil, Doré," Manmi used to say. Well, truth is, I'm in love with an obfuscation programme.

I'd met dj gruv grrl at Tony Roma's in Roppongi the week between Christmas and New Year's. I fell in love with her before the night was over.

She was my first. She was my only. And to this day, she's still the loveliest programme narrative I have ever seen.

My plan had been to go into Naeve Spencer's nexus with guns blazing, true Doré style: custom-made hot-pink AMT Hardballer Longslides. Glammed-up silver-dyed kink curls. Golden-brown skin oiled to a light sheen. Sleek, dark sunglasses. Black leather halter, black leather pants, black leather calf boots. Bad attitude.

Armstrong would watch my six. Mud holes would be stomped. Obfuscation codes would be broken. Naeve Spencer, the first gynoid that man has ever known, would be arrested for the murder of Manford Sutton, her creator.

Or so I thought.

I'd lost Armstrong going through the nexus, but more about him later. I also lost my Hardballers and black leather, but I'd anticipated that. I'd queued up takeover bots to storm Naeve Spencer's front porch thirty minutes after my entry. For all I know, they're still waiting outside Tony Roma's. If dj gruv grrl ever lets them in, they should order the baby back ribs with Sapporo Black.

See, what I hadn't anticipated was Naeve Spencer's front-porch programme not being hostile.

When I walked into Tony Roma's, dj gruv grrl and her crew was having filet mignon and piña coladas to kick off her first gig in Japan later that night at Matte Black. dj gruv grrl hadn't touched her piña colada and had only eaten a sliver of her filet mignon because she was about to spin the biggest set of her life and was determined not to get sick on the turntables.

Her crew was these three Israeli hostesses with trè bèl olive skin, gray-green eyes, and brown hair down to the middle of their backs: Michaela, Gabriela, and Isabela. The narrative went that dj gruv grrl had met them at the Shinagawa immigration office while they were renewing their entertainment visas.

Vrèman vre—truth be told—they're interference programmes. Part of the obfuscation. Their job is to distract infiltration programmes, like the black leather one I'd coded and wore. And they're damn good at it, too. I should know.

It helps that they're bèl ti fi yo. Drop dead. All three of them. Throw in a London-born, Filipino-Chinese-Japanese DJ expat with full lips, killer cheekbones, and oh-so-sexy black cat-eye glasses, and I was all aflutter with warmth, shyness, and excitement.

dj gruv grrl had asked me to join them because her girls were craving Krenglish. They were sick of slurred, wet, alcohol-saturated conversations and tired of pretending their lecherous clients didn't have bad breath, bad teeth, or both.

I knew prog bait when I saw it. I just chose to ignore it. Manmi had always said I was special. Manmi had always said I was a lesbian.

I didn't get to say much, though, because Michaela, Gabriela, and Isabela couldn't shut up about how their little hottie with Cantonese inflections underneath an Emma Peel accent turned down a scholarship at Julliard to be the next DJ Beauty, not the next Lera Auerbach. Whoever that is.

All I know is dj gruv grrl's sophisticated programme narrative made my nipples hard. And that was before she touched me.

We didn't stay long at Tony Roma's because dj gruv grrl's nervous energy had been getting the best of her. On the cold walk over to Matte Black—me toting her crate of twelve-inch vinyl, Michaela, Gabriela, and Isabela bringing up the rear—dj gruv grrl asked to put her hands in the slash pockets of my gray heather double-breasted wool Spiewak Jasper pea coat to keep those long, tapered, and delicate fingers of hers warm so they didn't seize up during her set.

I'd never seen a programme narrative with so much attention to detail. Like I said, sophisticated.

M lage l. I let her, of course. Even if it was a bit awkward with her walking behind me like that down the crowded sidewalks, cheek pressed against my right shoulder blade. I'd just wanted to hear that Emma Peel accent vibrate through my back.

Once we reached Matte Black—which I found out later was Naeve Spencer's pleasure centre—dj gruv grrl asked me to stay for her gig. Her cheeks had blazed scarlet from the cold and excitement beneath those cat-eye glasses of hers as she waited for my answer.

I couldn't have said no to save my life. Manford Sutton's software interpretation programme was spot on with his articulation of the emotional and behavioral profiles of my infiltration programme. Not even the Law Guild shrinks know about my fetish for eyewear and twentieth-century British women in catsuits.

dj gruv grrl's set was short, but the music was good; Michaela, Gabriela, and Isabela had to keep picking my jaw up off the floor. Her programme narrative said she'd spun old-school Chicago house music: Steve "Silk" Hurley, Farley "Jackmaster" Funk, Frankie Knuckles.

Music that made Michaela, Gabriela, and Isabela shake out their long hair and shimmy slim hips wrapped in low-slung jeans. Music that made them run their hands through my silver kink curls and put their hands on the byen seksi hips Manmi gave me.

I gibbered like a bag lady wearing four coats in summer while pushing a bashed-up shopping cart when dj gruv grrl found me after her set waiting for her in one of the ambient-lit rabbit warrens on the upper level of the club. And I don't gibber. I'll be the first to admit: Manford Sutton is the best programmer in all of Chicago. A coding genius.

But I didn't know the half of it.

Two hours into cozy margaritas with dj gruv grrl, a holo construct of Naeve Spencer popped up out of nowhere across the all of a sudden now-crammed-full room. She was surrounded by an international entourage of sycophantic beautiful people.

When the acoustics were just right, I could hear them kissing her ass in Kreyòl Ayisyen, Urdu, Kiswahili, Português, Íslenska, Bahasa Malaysia, and Hebrew. That's right, even my three new friends were puckering up.

That was when dj gruv grrl, with her cheeks still blazing scarlet, asked me if I wanted to go back to her apartment in Nakano. So I asked her if Blanford Sutton had programmed Naeve Spencer to get off on murder, sledgehammers, and blood splatter.

See, twelve hours before, two of my colleagues had found Manford Sutton naked on his bed in his Lake Shore Drive condo with his face and knees beaten to the consistency of baby food. Nearby was a bloody sledgehammer and a female android—a gynoid.

The very same gynoid who just happens to look, talk, and walk like Blanford Sutton's dead girlfriend, Naeve Spencer. The very same Naeve Spencer who died as a passenger in the car crash Manford Sutton had last summer in Japan. The very same car crash Japanese authorities blamed on a blowjob. The very same blowjob Blanford Sutton believes belonged to him.

My boys in Forensics concluded Manford Sutton was murdered right before gynoid Naeve Spencer's bio-electric battery, which lasts about a year, wound down. Thing is, she was five days past her expiration date. My boys also found traces of Manford Sutton's semen in her, and they found pills with the Manford Sutton logo on them in his medicine cabinet that enhanced his semen with fructose, lipids, and proteolytic enzymes to power the gynoid's bio-electric battery long past wind down.

They didn't find any trace of Blanford Sutton, though.

And they won't. L'al fè wout li. He's gone. Ghost. Out.

Blanford Sutton might be a coding genius, but li pa sòt. He ain't stupid. As good as he is, Blanford Sutton knows there's someone out there better.

Like me.

Which brings us back to dj gruv grrl, Naeve Spencer, and her nexus.

M pa vle kite. I didn't want to leave it. I didn't want to jack out.

I wanted to keep my BCID—my brain-computer interface device—slotted in my right temple port forever. I wanted to curl up under the covers with dj gruv grrl at her Nakano apartment until Blanford Sutton figures out how to make my realtime co-mingle with Naeve Spencer's nexus-time. And then I wanted to curl up with dj gruv grrl some more.

I didn't want to go back to the real world.

But first, I had to know if Naeve Spencer killed Manford Sutton. My Law Guild training demanded an answer. The forensic detective in me craved it.

Instead of answering my question right then and there, though, dj gruv grrl said she'd tell me everything I wanted to know about how Blanford Sutton dropped a li'l somethin'-somethin' in Naeve Spencer's code to make her 100 percent proficient with a sledgehammer—but in the morning, while I soaped her back in the shower. My last glimpse of Michaela, Gabriela, and Isabela was them leading the beautiful people in a dirty martini toast to Naeve Spencer.

On the walk to dj gruv grrl's place, we did all those things two young gaijin in Japan do when stumbling home drunk to fuck each other. We sniggered and pointed at the fully suited salarymen passed out on the sidewalk in their piss and vomit. We sang karaoke songs off-key at the top of our lungs. We shared our first kiss—sloppy, wet, and warm.

And then we saw the man in the middle of the road with his dick in one hand and a gun in the other.

He'd looked the perfect picture of the drunk, overworked Japanese businessman—dark rumpled suit; pristine white shirt; notched tie skewed to one side—except, he had his dick in one hand and a gun in the other.

The closer we got, the better we could see the one hand going fast enough to chafe himself raw. But when the salaryman looked up at us, we could also see he wasn't a salaryman at all. He was Armstrong. He pointed the gun at us.

"Don't move," he'd said. "Let me just make myself presentable."

Armstrong turned. We heard his zipper go up. When he turned back to us, his pants were open and he was holding himself again.

Three more times he turned to zip himself. Three more times he faced us with his dick in his hand. After the third time, Armstrong gave up trying, a pained look of disgust and humiliation on his face. Blanford Sutton's articulation of Armstrong's infiltration programme and behavior profile was a bitch.

That was when I first learned my girl didn't play. dj gruv grrl didn't take no shit from nobody. In Naeve Spencer's nexus, she was god and goddess, Lucifer and Lilith. Law Guild takeover bots and hot shit Law

Guild detectives didn't gain access to Naeve Spencer's most intimate place because dj gruv grrl forbade them. Even the good Law Guild detectives like Armstrong.

She had known he would try to return with a better infiltration programme when she kicked his ass out of the nexus, so dj gruv grrl used him to send the Law Guild, the rest of my infiltration team, and me a message.

dj gruv grrl snatched Armstrong's piece from him before he could try to tuck himself back in his pants again, put it in my hand, and told me:

"Here are your choices. Shoot him in the head and become one of Naeve Spencer's beautiful people. Or die a quick, painful death."

I'd blinked at her. "What?"

"I thought you'd say that," she'd said. She wasn't smiling. "How about this: I don't like to share. You can just be all mine. Michaela, Gabriela, and Isabela were, once."

"And what happens if I don't become your bitch?" I'd asked her. "You do me like Armstrong?"

"No." In three quick strides dj gruv grrl was in my face, all of five-foot-nothing, ox horns quivering, eyes fierce. "Put a fucking bullet in his brain"—she'd jabbed a finger at Armstrong—"or I send you back to the world and your cancer eats you alive in less than a week."

It was a struggle to keep the surprise off my face, but I'd had to fake some sort of genuine-looking response or she'd know my next words were a lie. So I went with my I-don't-know-what-the-fuck-you're-talking-about face, and told her:

"I don't have cancer."

dj gruv grrl could smell the bullshit, despite my Oscar-worthy performance.

"Bullshit," she'd said. "Remember when your nipples got nice and hard earlier tonight because you were so fascinated by the complexity of my programme narrative?" dj gruv grrl smirked and poked my left boob. "That was me disabling your cell division inhibitors and allowing the acceleration of your cancer cells to proliferate once again."

When I was three years old, Manmi moved to La Petite Haïti in Chicago from La Petite Haïti in Miami because some kaka bèf doktè told her he could send her stage-four breast cancer into complete remission. Nine months later, Manmi was dead.

On my twenty-fifth birthday, my doctor diagnosed me with meta-static breast cancer. He'd said I have six months to live. That was five months ago.

So, I got a second opinion from Dr. Émérentienne Célestin at the Tuskegee North Institute. She designed, developed, and built the Cell-Div NHBT implant to significantly slow the growth of cancer cells. A month after my first appointment, she put one in both breasts.

dj gruv grrl had taken my face in her hands. "Kounye a, at this very moment, you don't have cancer. There is no cancer in the nexus."

Her voice had been soft. Husky. I couldn't tell if she was trying to persuade me or seduce me or both. Whichever one, it worked.

I'd walked over to Armstrong. Leveled his piece at his head. He'd looked me in the eye. His fly had still been open. Big fat tears had rolled down his cheeks.

"Doré. Please," he'd begged me. "Don't do this."

I'd wanted to tell him to run. To flee Naeve Spencer's nexus, take off his code, and never come back.

But instead I'd said, "Kè m fè m mal anpil pou sa." I am very sorry for this.

And then I pulled the trigger. And when Armstrong fell to the ground, blood streaming out the middle of his forehead, I pulled the trigger again—onetwothreefourfivesix times—until the clip was empty. Dead nexus-time. Dead realtime.

dj gruv grrl took the gun from my hand. "We do Tony Roma's Thursday nights. Make sure you wear your black leather and those come-fuck-me boots."

And then she'd continued up the road, those lovely boyish hips of hers swaying back and forth, until she was just a pair of tight white jeans fading into the darkness.

So I did the only thing I could do. I followed.

Why wouldn't I? I refuse to let cancer take me.

Besides, I look damn good in those boots.

Long Time Lurker, First Time Bomber

You step into The Black Hand Side and never see coming the smack upside the back of your head.

"Girl, didn't I tell yo' narrow ass if you come up in here agin I was gone snatch a knot in yo' head?"

Big Mama Black has a heavy hand. Tears come to your eyes. The cowl of your lurksuit is seamless. It is tight. It is thin. It is sensitive. It is bonded to you by SoulSkin. It does not offer much protection.

"I'm sorry, Big Mama Black," you tell her, "but I'm looking for Roshan. Do you happen to know where he is?"

Big Mama Black puts her hands on her hips and twists her mouth as she looks down her nose at you. She does not like you. She has never liked you. She will never like you.

"You juss tryin' to start some mo' mess, is what you—"

"No—"

"Girl, you bet not interrupt me agin."

You dip your perfect round head and hide behind your long lashes, but only for a second. You do not want Big Mama Black to think you are being flippant or disrespectful by not looking her in the eye.

"I'm sorry, Big Mama Black." You do your best to make certain your voice is even and deferential.

Big Mama Black kisses her teeth. "Naw, you ain't sorry. I can see it in yo' eyes. If you was sorry, you wouldn't be up in my shop right now. If you was sorry, the first thing you would have said when you brought yo' narrow behind up in here is, 'Big Mama Black, I know you done said I cain't step foot up in here no mo', an' I'm sorry fo' disobeyin' you on that matter, but I juss got to git out there an' start some mo' mess agin, so that's why I'm here.' Right?"

You do not know how to answer that question, so you go with what you believe to be the safest answer. The answer that will leave Big Mama Black less inclined to smack you upside your head again.

"Yes ma'am, Big Mama Black," you say after an almost-too-long pause.

"You ain't even payin' attention to me right now, is you?"

You do not know how to answer that question, either. But you cannot lie. Big Mama Black is the world's best lie detector. She has caught you in every lie you have ever told her since you were five years old. She has even caught you in the lies you did not tell yet.

"No ma'am," you say, and you try not to wince as you brace for the smack upside your head. You fail. The smack does not come.

"Mmm hmm. I knew it."

Big Mama Black checks the digital readout of a cryo-box attached to the wall on the biotech half of her shop. It contains organic black silicon solar cells for sale.

"Like I said, you juss here to start some mo' mess." Big Mama Black makes an adjustment to the cryo-box's environment with a few taps of the keypad. "Ain't you done enough of that already? Ain't you kilt enough people?"

The skin on your face tightens. Your jaw clenches. Your ear canals constrict. Your forehead sweats. Your cheeks get oily. The shop sounds as if it is underwater. The door to The Black Hand Side slams open. You flinch.

Two solarpunks stumble into the waiting room. A young girl and a young boy. Your arms are trembling. The young girl and the young boy look to be your age. Your legs are trembling. The young girl has her arm around the young boy's waist. You want to sit down. The young boy has his arm around the young girl's shoulders. You need to sit down. The young boy leans against the young girl. His legs have buckled. Your legs want to buckle. His toes drag across the marble floor. Your tear drops onto the marble floor.

Big Mama Black has never said anything like that to you before.

Big Mama Black helps the young girl get the young boy into a waiting room chair. You wipe the tears from your eyes. No more shall fall.

"Chile," Big Mama Black says to the young girl, putting the back of her hand on the young boy's forehead, "you slam open my door like that agin an' I'm gone make sure you cain't sit down fo' a week."

The young girl, like you, is tall. She, like you, is strong. She, like you, is twenty-two years old. And she, like you, believes with all of her heart Big Mama Black will take a switch to her if she does that again. You can see it in her eyes.

"I'm sorry, Big Mama Black," the young girl says, "but something wrong with Niko."

"'Somethin' ain't wrong with him." Big Mama Black looks at her receptionist and nods, once. "He is what's wrong with him. What was the first thing I tol' y'all when y'all came up in here last month for them solar cell implants?"

"Don't wait too long to upload our stored solar energy." The young girl squeezes Niko's hand.

"Why?" Big Mama Black asks. The receptionist hands Big Mama Black a sheaf of cool-down strips.

"Because the unprocessed excess energy can make us sick." Two tears roll down the young girl's cheeks and plop onto Niko's hand.

"How?" Big Mama Black crouches in front of Niko, sticks a cool-down strip on his forehead, and then motions for the young girl to remove his shirt.

"Our accumulator can only store so much solar energy. It's a delicate organ. The excess energy spreads throughout our body and becomes infused into our cells." The young girl says this with a practiced and measured cadence.

"And then what happens?" Big Mama Black raises Niko's arms and gives two cool-down strips to the young girl.

"Our body temperature rises. We sweat. We overheat. We fall into a coma. We die." The young girl places the cool-down strips within Niko's armpits, adhering them to the coarse, dark hair there.

"You die." Big Mama Black clucks her tongue and shakes her head. "Y'all either hard-headed, stupid, or both, 'cause I cain't get mo' straightforward than that."

Two more tears quiver on the young girl's round chin before they drop to the floor. Big Mama Black's eyes soften for a moment and she pats the young girl's hand.

"Chile, I know you ain't stupid," Big Mama Black says, her voice less mama bear now, "'cause if you was, you wouldn't be here. You lit up from within. You beautiful. You a sunchild. You a solar. That's the smartest choice you could have ever made in your life." Big Mama Black flicks you a gaze and her eyes go hard. When she turns back to the young girl, her eyes are soft again. "But it's gon' be all right. Big Mama Black gon' make it all better."

Big Mama Black stands. Her knees crack like rifle shots. Two male nurses appear at her side. One helps Niko through a door leading to an examination room.

"Now, go on in the back with that knucklehead boyfriend of yours to one of them repair an' relax solariums so y'all can get better. By the looks of you, yo' accumulator juss about full too." Big Mama Black gives the remaining cool-down strips to one of the nurses. "And Inaya?"

The young girl turns back to Big Mama Black before following Niko through the door. "Yes, ma'am?"

"I bet not see you or him up in here like that ever agin."

"Never agin, ma'am."

Big Mama Black sighs and turns to you. There is no trace of softness in her eyes now.

"You out there in Chicago, runnin' roun' that godforsaken city-state, startin' wars that was long finished for this sorry State we live in 'cause they too scairt or too smart to do it themselves. Pro'lly both." Big Mama Black kisses her teeth. "You doin' the Devil's work, an' don't even know he whisperin' in yo' ear."

"Now, Big Mama Black, I—"

You do not see that smack upside your head coming, either.

You rub the back of your beautiful, curved head. The smarting pain is combined and magnified by the pain receptors in the thin layer of your SoulSkin and the pain receptors in the epidermis and dermis of your real skin. Your SoulSkin stings. The back of your head stings. More tears come to your eyes. You tell yourself these tears are because of Roshan and not Big Mama Black.

And you are still telling yourself lies.

"Chile, I ain't yo' mammy, an' I ain't yo' gran'mammy, but if you take that tone wit me agin, I'm gon' make you go out back an' cut me a switch off of that birch tree an' whoop you like you done stole a Mississippi mule."

You open your mouth to speak, and then close it. It is the smartest thing you have done since you killed your boyfriend in a terrorist attack.

0 0 0

You are not a terrorist. You do not love Roshan.

This was your morning prayer. It was your half-day mantra. It was your nighttime hoodoo charm.

But you did not believe it.

And yet, you cleaved to it. You clutched it close. You chanted it for resolve. You chanted it for strength. You chanted it for courage.

But on the day you killed Roshan, your words fell from your mouth and dribbled onto the ground like warm, fat raindrops on a summer afternoon.

You wanted to get down on your hands and knees, put your lips to the hot, sandy concrete, and suck the moisture back into your mouth before it sizzled away. You wanted to form the words again and speak them with confidence that one time.

But it was too late. Those words did not matter anymore.

You had placed the bomb. You had identified your escape route. You had less than three minutes to get as far away from Oak Street Beach as you could. And you had to go through more than 100,000 people to do it.

And then, in the light of green and purple and yellow Venn diagram flower bursts overhead, you saw Roshan.

He should not have been there. You knew he would be there. Your chant made him be there.

Your lurksuit collected enough photons from the dim light of your surroundings to shift you from the shadows of the nearest Beachstro Restaurant gazebos and expose your hiding spot. A woman eating grilled chicken cavatappi with spinach, cremini mushrooms, and sun-dried tomatoes in the gazebo on your left startled at your sudden appearance. She yipped. She flung a sliced mushroom at your feet. She peed herself a little.

You pushed through the white and brown and black and bronze arms and legs and shoulders and hips toward Roshan. Some people stumbled. Some people fell. Some people yelped. Some people cursed.

They would not get out of your way fast enough.

"Zèl."

Your Haitian Creole pronunciation was passable. Your lurksuit shed photons and the shadows rushed back to you in response to your whisper. Enormous ragged black wings unfurled behind you. They rose twelve feet above your head. Your hands flexed, ready to rend. You screeched. You raged. A thin thread of saliva stretched top to bottom within your wide-open mouth.

The people around you recoiled, ran, tripped, fell, trampled, screamed—

"Rakaya?"

And then, Roshan was in front of you.

A champagne flute had lain broken at his feet. The sand was wet and stained dark in places. You hoped it was not blood. Roshan's boys stood behind him, disheveled. They all wore tight, black ribbed tank tops. They all wore wrinkled, black linen shorts. They all wore casual black leather loafers. They all looked scared as hell.

Roshan cupped your face in his large, soft hands. His eyes showed worry as he looked down at you. His smooth, dark, bald head gleamed from implanted solar cells, reflecting a quick succession of red and blue and white fireworks from the night sky.

"We have to go we have to go we have to go we have to go," you told him.

"Are you OK?" Roshan searched you for injury, but his hands stayed on your face.

Your lurksuit gobbled more photons until your harpy wings faded. You grabbed his wrists and started to pull him away from the beach, away from Lake Michigan, toward the Red Line, toward the L train, toward home, toward safety—

But you were too late.

Arusha Donta, Manyara Donta, and Karatu Donta surged forward. You had not seen their HUAW position, where they had lain in wait. You had not seen their approach. You had not seen them coming for you.

They were quick. They were fast. They were tall. They were wide. They were zaftig class.

You were surprised by their agility. You did not know zaftig class could move like that. You had heard they have heavy-plated Maybach Exelero exo-skeletons fused to their bodies. You expected them to amble along on their massive legs like the lumbering pachydermata their exo-skeletons were designed to resemble.

But they did not.

Arusha Donta, Manyara Donta, and Karatu Donta charged the crowd. Full speed. Three-hundred-plus pounds of bulk. Most of the crowd had been appreciating the fireworks. Most of the crowd had their chins tipped toward the sky. Most of the crowd had perished without knowing who or what hit them.

But you knew. You saw.

You saw Arusha Donta break their backs with her massive feet. You saw Manyara Donta crush their chests with her massive fists. You saw Karatu Donta split their stomachs with his massive tusks. Men. Women. Children. Old and young. Healthy and infirmed.

They committed these atrocities so they could get to you. They committed these atrocities so they could protect you. They committed these atrocities so they could save you.

And they did.

You act as if you do not remember this. You act as if this is your first time hearing this. You act as if you are stunned by this.

Do not be. They were hired from the Mercenaries Guild to protect you at all costs. They were hired from the Mercenaries Guild to protect you by any means necessary. Just as you have vowed to destroy the city-state of Chicago by any means necessary.

Seconds before the bomb you planted exploded, Arusha Donta, Manyara Donta, and Karatu Donta surrounded you. They hunched down. They were careful with their strength. They were careful with their bulk. They were careful with their tusks.

They pressed against you. They embraced you. They shielded you.

You did not see the explosion. You did not feel the explosion. You did not hear the explosion.

All you saw was their metallic matte-black skin. All you felt was their cold metallic matte-black skin against your cheeks. And all you heard was Arusha Donta's clear soprano voice through the curve of her metallic matte black belly.

She had sung:

When this world is over,
It will come again,
Formed of hate, formed of evil, formed of carnal sin.
When this world returns,

Fire will give it purity,
Hatred and greed will burn,
Of that is a surety.

And when Arusha Donta, Manyara Donta, and Karatu Donta released you from their embrace, giving you back to the world, you saw your blessing of purity. The beach burned. Three hundred and fifty-six people burned. Roshan burned.

Oily, orange, and black.

0 0 0

"That boy ain't been the same since you kilt him."

Big Mama Black has an audience on the spa side of her shop now: Ms. Irene, Ms. Elaine, and Ms. Savannah Mae. All three solar women look at you. All three solar women frown at you. All three solar women kiss their teeth at you.

You flop into a chair beside them. You keep your promise. No tears fall in front of these dignified yet gossipy women. But you are tired.

"He shouldn't be the same. He's a Blanford Sutton Industries android now."

The shop goes quiet. Spa side and biotech side. You did not mean to take that tone. It is a good thing Big Mama Black is on the biotech side of the shop, or another knot would have been snatched upside your head.

"One of y'all better tell this heifer that ain't how you talk to grown folk, or I'm gone come over there an' remind her."

Big Mama Black does not look at you. You do not look at her. It is better this way. You are sure of it. You would wither under her cut eye in every sense of the word, including the literal one.

Your over-sized, long-sleeved white linen shirt would strip away. Your loose, white linen pants would strip away. Your lurksuit would strip away. Your SoulSkin would strip away. Your real skin would strip away. Your bones would turn black. They would shrivel. They would crumble. They would blow away.

So instead, you look at Ms. Elaine, Ms. Irene, and Ms. Savannah Mae. They do not pardon your insolence, however.

Ms. Elaine kisses her teeth again and turns a page of the glossy magazine she is reading. "Look like somebody gettin' too big for her britches."

Ms. Irene takes a peppermint from her purse, unwraps it, and puts it in her mouth. "I got somethin' to fix that."

Ms. Savannah Mae shakes her head and then gives your lurksuit cowl the side-eye. "That girl ain't gon' feel yo' switch through her catsuit."

Ms. Elaine cackles, quite tickled by Ms. Savannah Mae's misnomer. "Girl, that ain't no catsuit. It's called a 'lurksuit.'"

Ms. Irene crosses her long, dark, lovely arms and rocks side-to-side. "I don't care what it's called. When I get 'hold of her, she ain't gon' be able to sit down fo' a week."

Ms. Savannah Mae crosses her long, dark, lovely legs and humphs. "I heard tell it's made of some special technology that keeps heat an' cold out while providin' light armor protection at the same time. That girl ain't gon' feel yo' switch through that."

Ms. Irene rolls her peppermint in her mouth. "Oh, truss me, she will." Ms. Irene rolls the right sleeve of her black T-shirt up over her deltoid. She flexes her bicep. You are surprised to see a fifty-some-thing-year-old woman with such muscle tone. She grins at Ms. Savannah Mae. "You ain't seen my switch arm lately."

Ms. Elaine leans across Ms. Savannah Mae, puts her hand on Ms. Irene's bare knee, and stage whispers in her ear: "We got church early tomorrow mornin', an' yo' friend Ms. Savannah Mae over here talkin' 'bout catsuits. You better tell her she need to get her mind out the gutter, an' get right wit God."

Ms. Irene pulls back from Ms. Elaine in mock offense. "Oh, so this heathen my friend now?"

Ms. Savannah Mae frowns at Ms. Elaine. "Honey, somebody tol' you wrong. I am right wit God."

Ms. Irene gives Ms. Elaine a knowing smile. "The way I remember it, you an' Ms. Savannah Mae used to run the streets on the South Side of Chicago e'ry Saturday night lookin' fo' juke joints to get yo' dance on, while I was at home, on my knees, sendin' up prayers to our Lord an' Savior Jesus Christ fo' y'all heathen souls."

The shop goes quiet again, this time for three beats. And then, Ms. Irene, Ms. Savannah Mae, and Big Mama Black burst out with cackles of girlish glee.

Ms. Elaine does not laugh. Her face is serious. Her voice is quiet. "I heard tell them lurksuits bonded wit SoulSkin, so the people wearin' them feel e'rything."

Ms. Irene leans into Ms. Savannah Mae this time, puts a hand on her bare knee, and stage whispers in her ear: "An' she mean e'rything. I heard tell Mr. Darnell bought Ms. Elaine one of them catsuits last Valentine's Day, which is how she know all 'bout the way they work."

Ms. Elaine looks up high at the ceiling and fans her eyes with both hands to prevent the coming tears from spilling down her cheeks. "No, I know how they work 'cause my gran'baby got one of them."

Ms. Elaine's voice is softer now. You almost cannot hear her, and you are sitting in the seat next to her.

"Which gran'baby? Marquis?" Ms. Savannah Mae asks Ms. Elaine.

Ms. Elaine nods, still fanning her eyes. "He one of them Assassin Guild members, like this gal over here." She means you. "They recruited him when he was six years old. Right after his good-fo'-nothin' daddy cut out on him an' his mama."

Ms. Irene shakes her beautiful, dark, bald head. "It ain't right fo' a guild like that, one of them shady guilds, to take our chirren so young. That sinful Thieves Guild doin' the same thing."

Big Mama Black shakes her beautiful, dark, bald head as she fusses with the vacutainers for brown sugar and honey exfoliant on the spa side of the shop. "Y'all can say they sinful all y'all want, but that guild ain't no diff'rent from ours."

Ms. Irene closes her eyes and raises both hands. "Preach, Sister Reverend."

Big Mama Black rolls her eyes at Ms. Irene's silliness. "We do the same here in the Energy Guild: We train up our babies when they young, startin' them wit solar cell implant surgery as soon as we think they can take it. The younger they are, the easier it is fo' them to learn 'bout them cells an' e'rything else they need to know 'bout bein' a solar." She casts her cut eye toward the back-room solariums where Inaya and Niko are receiving treatment. "Take some of them longer to learn than others, though."

Ms. Elaine shakes her beautiful, dark, bald head. "Juss 'cause that's the way we do it don't make it right, though. An' neither does all that money the Assassins Guild gave my baby girl in exchange fo' my gran'baby. I ain't seen him in six years. I wouldn't know what he looked like if he walked past me on the street. His mama wouldn't, neither."

Ms. Irene stands, shoos you out of your seat, sits next to Ms. Elaine, and takes Ms. Elaine's left hand into her own. "We all slaves to the Guild. E'ry last one of us."

Ms. Savannah Mae takes Ms. Elaine's right hand into her own. "Why didn't you tell us 'bout this?"

Ms. Elaine shrugs, and then lets out a big, shaky sigh. "Ain't no gran'mother in this world gon' tell her best friends that her gran'baby a terrorist an' her daughter sold him to Guild like a slave owner."

"I am not a terrorist." The words leap out of your mouth and onto the marble floor before you realize you have spoken them. They hiss their sonorant and sibilant consonants with a confident but defensive measured cadence. "We are not terrorists."

Ms. Savannah Mae takes a sip of her complimentary peppermint tea. "That may be the case, but you fo' damn sure a mass murderer."

Ms. Elaine licks a finger and turns another page of her magazine. "Ain't no two ways 'bout that."

Big Mama Black fusses with the vacutainers of homemade shea butter whip moisturizer. "Funny how the State of Illinois gives you millions to kill 357 people who ain't done a damn thing to you—includin' my heart, my boy, my son—but when somebody call you out on it, you an' Webster's Dictionary cain't agree on the definition of the word 'terrorist.'"

You stop yourself from looking up at the ceiling and fanning your eyes. "I paid for—"

Ms. Savannah Mae waves you silent. "Chile, we all know you paid fo' that boy's funeral, you paid fo' his conversion into a Blanford Sutton Industries android, an' you paid fo' his psychiatrist after he woke up. We been in the know 'bout him, you, an' e'rything y'all done since Ol' Heck was a pup. They don't call us The Three Whispers fo' nothin'."

Ms. Irene points to the spa side front door in a vague direction of Blanford Sutton Industries. "But what The Three Whispers don't know is why them fake human cells Blanford Sutton gave Roshan ain't playin' nice wit them new solar cells Big Mama Black implanted in him. That boy losin' money on his solar energy upload left, right, an' center."

"Speakin' of money..." Big Mama Black gives Ms. Elaine a complimentary cup of peppermint tea. "How much you take fo' that Oak Street Beach contract from the State of Illinois? Ten million? Fifty million? One hundred million? 'Cause we know it was a lot. You was able to pay fo' Roshan's conversion an' have money left over fo' renovations to yo' house."

Big Mama Black knows better than this. She is from the old school. She is from a time when people did not stick their noses into other people's business. She is from a place where it was rude to ask people about their salary and money, unless the topic was broached first. Her mama taught her better than that. Her mama's mama taught her better than that.

"Mama, you know better to ask a question like that."

Her son knows better than that.

You turn and see Roshan standing behind you on the biotech side of the shop. You want to run to him. You want to jump on him and hug him and kiss him and apologize to him—

Instead, you do nothing. You say nothing.

Roshan walks past you to the spa-side entrance of the shop. "I need some sun. And some privacy. Let's talk outside."

0 0 0

Big Mama Black does not care you tried your best to make sure Roshan would not be at Oak Street Beach that night. Roshan does not care you tried your best to make sure he would not be at Oak Street Beach that night. Only *you* care you tried your best to make sure Roshan would not be at Oak Street Beach that night.

But you did not try hard enough.

That is what they are thinking at this very moment.

The good thing is, I know your thoughts. You know my thoughts. We are forever connected.

I am your lurksuit. I am the paragon of black market Haitian Creole technology. I am the interface between you and your SoulSkin. I am your millions of synapses. I am your trillions of electrical and chemical nerve impulses. I am your manifested speed of thought. We live and die by your thought and my action.

But today, right now, I have a wonderful idea.

I can speak your thoughts. I can speak my thoughts. I can speak the right thoughts. I can make Roshan love us again.

He still loves us now. I mean, he still loves me now. He is just upset. Hurt. Confused. And maybe afraid.

See, that I cannot understand. I cannot understand how you do not understand Roshan has stopped loving you. Humans can fall in love with someone, just as humans can fall out of love with someone. Time can end love. Death can end love. Betrayal can end love.

I don't believe that. People can't fall out of love. Once you love someone, you love them, in one way or another, forever. People don't turn love on and off like a faucet.

Roshan is not people. He is a Blanford Sutton android. And being transformed into a Blanford Sutton android can end love.

Do not mistake me, though; you made the right choice. You should have paid for Roshan's conversion into an android. You should have paid to have all of his memories extracted and downloaded into his new body. And you should have kept that most painful memory intact.

Otherwise, how would he trust you again? How would he love you again?

You know this will not be easy, eske se pa sa? Roshan may never pick up his love and give it to you again. Are you prepared if he does not? You should be prepared if he does not. And you should not be surprised if he does not.

Everything I did, every action I took, every decision I made was for love.

Love of Roshan, or love of the State?

(...)

See, that is why we are having this conversation now. You cannot hesitate when Roshan asks you these kinds of questions when you join him outside The Black Hand Side in a few moments. Were I him, and you hesitated like that with me, even if it were just 0.6 seconds, I would have turned, walked away without another word, and you would never see me again.

You don't understand. I—

I do not understand? Did you truly just say I do not understand? If anyone understands your actions, your machinations, your orchestrations—your calculated decisions—it is I.

I understand why you invited Roshan to spend the week of the twelfth of August at your place. The weatherman had said there would be an extreme heat warning that week. The window-mounted air conditioner in your bedroom was old. Loud. Decrepit. It coughed, dry and hard, like an old man with emphysema.

The central air conditioning in Roshan's house is efficient. Powerful. Quiet. It is the dry, cool touch of desert twilight on skin. But you knew he would stay with you. You knew Roshan would endure pain and suffering for you. You knew he could not resist you.

He loved the taste of your sweat in the hollows of your collarbones. He loved the taste of your sweat in the crooks of your elbows. He loved the taste of your sweat on the backs of your knees.

But he could only taste you and love you for so long.

You know that's not fair.

His stamina was fleeting.

You know that's a side effect of the humidity.

His muscles pained him.

You know that's a symptom of his solar sickness.

His mood was unpleasant.

(...)

Silence. The passive assent.

You cannot be defensive like that when you speak with Roshan. If you are, he will turn and walk away. I would turn and walk away, and I am your lurksuit.

You must remember why you are here at The Black Hand Side. You must remember why you have endured Big Mama Black's smacks. You cannot waver. You cannot falter. You cannot hesitate.

If you must, remember those special moments you and Roshan shared to bolster your confidence. For example, remember when you and Roshan were little and Big Mama Black would not let him play outside on days the humidity was higher than sixty percent? The cloying, moist air would filter through the outer layer of his solar cells on those days. Water vapor would form. The condensation would become trapped.

Roshan would become irritable. Sluggish. Cranky. He would stay in bed all day. And where were you? Beside his bed. All day. In the exact place a best friend should be.

He should also remember that. He has those memories. He

shares those memories. You made sure of it. Mention it. Use it to your advantage.

That feels wrong. Dirty. Immoral. As if I'm manipulating him.

You are. I thought you realized this, considering—

I'm done with that.

Take pride in that.

(...)

Rakaya, I tell you this with the utmost of admiration: You executed a masterstroke of genius on the morning of the twelfth of August. You played Roshan like Beethoven's Violin Concerto in D Major, and I do not mean this in a negative way.

How can I take that in any way but—

I am ignoring that to remind you Roshan wanted to taste the salty warmness in the hollows of your collarbones and the crooks of your elbows and on the backs of your knees as you lay in bed that morning. He did not want to roll away from you and pull the sheet over his head. He did not realize you had brought about those conflicting reactions.

And why would he? Roshan had responded in the very same way to humidity ever since he was five years old. Ever since his mother agreed to have the State of Illinois implant solar cells just beneath his skin at the University of Illinois at Urbana-Champaign. Ever since Ford Heights and the Chicagoland area got 0.3 percent hotter in summer and 0.5 percent more humid in August.

For him, this was just chronic illness.

Don't you think it's sinister and cruel and treacherous I did that to him?

I said you were a genius, not some Sunday afternoon holo-vid supervillain. Listen: In this case, the end justifies the means.

But in the end, Roshan died.

Think positive. In a new beginning, Roshan is waiting for you outside in the warm sunshine right now.

(He remembers me blowing him to bits.)

No; he remembers you helping him to push through his pain and discomfort throughout the years. He remembers you lying in bed with him when you were teenagers, reading *Brown Girl in the Ring* and *Parable of the Sower* and *Who Fears Death* to him. He remembers you whispering, "dekolte." He remembers your lurksuit retracting below the waist. He remembers your exposed SoulSkin. He remembers you pressing your naked hip against him.

He remembers being content with you.

I remember his sun-starved solar cells devouring the ATP within his mitochondria. I remember making him poached eggs and hash browns and bacon in the morning to drive away his lethargy.

I remember him dragging himself out of my bed, pulling on a tight, black ribbed tank top and black shorts, pushing through his discomfort and pain, and going to see his mother at The Black Hand Side.

I remember him wanting his mother's food, his mother's love, and his mother's healing.

My love didn't heal him. My love didn't comfort him. My love didn't restore him.

And he remembers returning to you a week later. He remembers climbing into your bed. He remembers hugging you up in apology for his too few kisses and his lack of stamina and his unpleasant mood.

Do you remember that? Do you remember hugging him back, kissing his dark, shimmery, bald head, pressing your naked hip against his muscular thigh, and doing things to him that his mother could not do?

Why are we bickering about this?

Why are you being so sullen and petulant and bitter about this? Why are you pretending you never loved Roshan? Why are you pretending you do not want him in your life anymore?

Sometimes, I wonder about you, Rakaya. I have intimate knowledge of how your mind works. I know you. You are not evil. You may not think of yourself as a terrorist, but you are. And you may not think you love Roshan, but you do.

I know this with every fiber of my being.

You could have moved Roshan out of the way on your chessboard of treachery the day of the 8-12 bombing in a more detached, straightforward manner.

Instead of inviting him to spend the week at your house, facilitating his debilitating illness, you could have dropped by his house and pointed to the blue skies overhead that fateful morning. You could have reminded him double-time upload rates were in effect because of the abundant sunshine. You could have told him it was the perfect day to sell his blackpower at The Black Hand Side. And you could have suggested he should spend some quality time with his mother. She had not seen him in a while.

You did not need to read to him or kiss his bald, shimmery head or retract the bottom of your lurksuit. His solar energy upload would have taken most of the day, and his rest and recovery from such a massive upload would have lasted through the night. You did not need to bond with him. You did not need to love him. You did not need to sicken him.

He would not have been at Oak Street Beach that night had you not intervened. Your meddling changed the course of his life.

Either way—

No. There is no either way. Just one way. My way. The only way. The fucked-up way. The way that got Roshan killed.

You did not kill Roshan. God killed Roshan. The Universe killed Roshan. The State of Illinois killed Roshan. The Sovereign State of Chicago killed Roshan. Roshan's boys killed Roshan.

Now, you're not making any sense.

And yet, you are?

Correct me if I am wrong, but you are not divine. You are not omnipotent. You are not omnipresent. You did not create life. You did not sit in a darkness that was not called dark and determine every thought, word, and action of every person on this planet at a time so far gone it did not know seconds.

You did not know Roshan would meet his boys at The Black Hand Side that morning and charm his mother into giving them a free rest and recovery boost so they could be at Oak Street Beach that night to ogle the scantily clad city-state girls.

Certain events are meant to transpire in the manner they do. The Sovereign State of Chicago was meant to be selfish and greedy. The State of Illinois was meant to be a champion for every city, town, and suburb in the Land of Lincoln. This long conflict between the two polities was meant to be a battle between good and evil.

Just as you were meant to be a terrorist.

Just as you were meant to love Roshan.

Just as Roshan was meant to love you.

So go get your boy. Tell him you love him. Tell him he loves you. And tell him you two will love each other forever.

0 0 0

Roshan basks in the sun, arms outstretched, eyes closed, face raised to the blue sky. His tight, black, ribbed tank top is minimal for maximum exposure. His tight, black solar shorts are minimal for maximum exposure. His solar cells do not gleam in the sunshine as they once did. His dark skin is no longer lovely. It looks bruised and soft, like fruit that is rotting and has gone off.

Tears come to your eyes. You did this to him.

"Do you remember everything?" you ask him in an almost-whisper.

"I remember enough." Roshan does not open his eyes. He does not drop his arms.

"I wanted you to remember everything."

"Did you want me to remember that?"

...

Why are you hesitating?! I told you not to hesitate when responding to him!

"No." Two tears fall to the hot concrete. "But I wanted you to trust me. You wouldn't have trusted me if I paid Blanford Sutton to have his coders delete that memory."

"I dream about you. I dream about that night. I dream in orange and black."

More tears fall to the hot concrete. "You probably won't believe me, but I don't sleep anymore, because when I do all I see is you on the sand, dead, broken, and burned."

"Why didn't you tell me you were a terrorist?"

"You knew. You saw my lurksuit. No noninitiate is supposed to see a lurksuit and live. You knew I was Shadow Guild. It was just a matter of you guessing Thieves Guild or Assassins Guild."

"But you didn't tell me. You didn't confide in me. We've known each other since we were five years old." His face is slack, without expression. You think of rotted fruit again.

"There was nothing to tell. I was an initiate. An acolyte of the Praying Hands. I hadn't killed anyone yet."

"Until me."

"Until you."

You wipe the tears from your cheeks. You touch his dark, smooth, muscled arm. The skin there is not warm. Not like it used to be when he basked in the sun.

"Do you love me?"

He opens his eyes. He drops his arms. He looks at you.

And you know. You have always known.

When Raf Used to be Ghetto

For about an hour, I'm genuinely polite to Ms. Edna Mae Hamilton. She'd always been my favorite babysitter, even if she smelled a little bit like lanolin. Last week, Mama told me she wanted to stay sharp, so she's studying Mandarin. At seventy-five years young today, I say to her, "Go 'head wit your bougie-level grammarin'!"

Now, some of y'all might think I'm insulting her or finding fault with her, but that's just me exalting her and maybe even forming a cult for her. And for good reason.

When Ms. Edna Mae looked after me, she taught me with exceptional alchemy her mastery of how to scramble eggs with a pinch of salt, pepper, and pure rhapsody. To this day, that's the only thing I can cook quite happily, and if I may say so myself, passably.

So, I'm cool with being at her birthday party, in all actuality. Even when she hugs me and kisses me and tells me how handsome I be, and how I should not tease my four stepsisters, please, and how she will shatter my stepfather's knees with a sledgehammer forged beneath all Seven Seas, which she will swing with strength and the greatest of ease, so he better treat my mother like the Queen of All Bees and start by taking her for at least two weeks in Belize.

My stepfather is in the kitchen, so we all know he heard that. But in case he didn't, Ms. Edna Mae will Blurb that. I keep quiet because I don't want to disturb that. Oh, shit, here we go; my stepfather responds and chirps that.

I'm not ready for Ms. Edna Mae's TruTell petty, so I go out to the porch where me and my boys can mean-mug stock images for Getty.

What? Don't look at me like I'm speaking Yeti. We all know they got sat-cams high up over the Serengeti moving around the world seventy-two times faster than the great Mario Andretti.

The first person I see is E. We knock shoulders hard enough to break boulders ensconced wit four-leaf clovers and change the formation of the White Cliffs of Dover.

"Sup, yo." He gives me a pound.

I look around to see who came down for Ms. Edna Mae's Birthday Get Down—one, two, three—I frown. They all here, except for that class clown, who been passed down by the Black Gowns since sundown at Fun Town. He know who I'm talkin' 'bout.

"Where Reese at?" I ask them.

"Tryin' to get him some pussy," Big Sherm says, feelin' no shame to blast him.

"Try is all he gon' do," Pretty Boy Blue adds, well on his quest to drag him.

We all laugh. Reese our boy, but that don't mean we can't slag him.

"From who?" I ask, genuinely wonderin' who would shag him. Pro'lly that quiet girl who always like to TruTell tag him.

"That bougie redbone 'round the corner on Crandon who parents tryin' to gentrify The Manor but ain't gettin' nowhere," Nate says, an' pantomime referee-flags him.

"Bougie-ass Naëma?" I ask him, tryin' not to laugh 'cause he got bad breath so bad she gon' have to gas mask him. "He ain't gon' bone her. He ain't redbone enough." Hollywood for damn sure wouldn't cast him.

"He been tryin' since right after y'all moved." E says the last part in a voice so small I might as well gagged him. Or even worse, just out of the blue smacked him.

To be straight up honest, I want to give him a pound, a shrug, a playful mean mug, and then say, "Sorry 'bout my parents, man," as I give him a hug.

But I don't.

Wait. Why am I apologizing for them? The decision to move me and my stepsisters to the North Shore was made by Mama and him, and not on a whim, but to escape the gangs, drugs, and other Jeffery Manor gems.

We all go quiet an' shift an' fidget on Ms. Edna Mae's porch, not sure what to say next. Then, my boys look at me. I don't think I ever seen them this vexed.

They look like they 'bout to flex pecs an' snap necks wit me bein' they next work project. Nah, man, I ain't 'bout to get wrecked, an' I for damn sure ain't about to jeopardize my cerebral cortex.

But it's too late. It's on an' already out the gate.

Big Sherm lands a feathery left jab on my chin. I counter with a light right to Big Sherm's temple an' my fist hits like a water vapor rollin' pin. Pretty Boy Blue grins as E spins the blow-by-blow wit Nate on color commentary to Big Sherm's annoyed chagrin.

But our impromptu play-fight boxin' match is over almost as soon as it begins: immediate an' wit the quickness 'cause Big Sherm gets serious agin.

"I see y'all done went an' got all uppity an' bougie on a nwafa." He kisses his teeth at our Conquest Knight XV in Ms. Edna Mae's driveway an' then look at me sideways.

I swear this motherfucker 'bout to find at least five ways of how not to give me high praise fo' my prodigal return to The Manor an' its wild ways.

But I ain't gon' be fazed. An' I for damn sure ain't gon' be dazed when my boys unleash they shade 'bout my cut-by-a-white-boy fade an' the grape Kool-Aid I made in the third grade that should have left most of they teeth decayed 'cause of my full-on sugar cavalcade.

But I'm gon' say it now: Don't y'all get played.

My boys gon' say they was so afraid that they prayed my drank wouldn't do them like nightshade, set it off like a hand grenade, or cut they insides easy, sharp, an' swift like a switchblade wielded by a drunk South Chicago bridesmaid.

But for real for real, they was all up in it, like it was a Kool-Aid drinkin' contest an' each of them was doin' they best to win it.

"Yo, y'all 'member when Raf used to be ghetto?" Nate asks almost depressedly, as if he misses the best of me and isn't happy with what he sees that's left of me.

"How old was he when this nwafa designed, sketched, an' built that Kool-Aid dispenser he hooked up to his mama's kitchen sink?" Big Sherm asks this almost aggressively, but wit such gravitas that maybe he thought that should have been my destiny: ghetto Kool-Aid dispenser magnate Rafa Carnegie.

"That nwafa was juss seven years old." Pretty Boy Blue says this cheerfully, wit all sorts of levity.

"But wait, y'all forgettin' the good part! Not only did that nwafa hook up a Kool-Aid dispenser to his mama's kitchen sink, but he made sure it came in two different flavors: red drank fo' the left knob, an' purple drank fo' the right knob." Nate says this almost breathlessly, an' we all know he gon' post that word-for-word on his social feeds suc-cessively fo' maximum hilarity.

"He was a smart motherfucker." Pretty Boy Blue says this wit no hint of jealousy.

"Was? Still is!" Big Sherm says this wit an air of definity.

"I bet he get straight A's an' he on the high honor roll or the dean's list or some shit." Pretty Boy Blue says this wit confident certainty.

"Yeah, at one of those good-ass, rich-ass white schools where they teach you to speak an' write in allegory, but make it mandatory, unless you really don't want to 'cause it's an elite an' exclusive Montessori."

E doesn't say that out loud, but his suss is clear and proud, as if all of a sudden he's a Stater avowed. Never would I have thought my best friend would suss about me in a InTell so wretchedly, and yet so professedly.

But I shouldn't be upset (or surprised). Stanford Sutton (South Side despised, and definitely not a saint like Blanford Sutton, who the Sovereign State has canonized) can use his omnipresent sensors (shady and disguised) to actuate anyone the way he wants (compromised and colonized).

Like wit my best friend. Which, if you ask me, is not a good blend, especially for Stanford Sutton, since this is Blanford Sutton's network and could be his end.

See, I never, ever wanted to know E's thoughts 'cause we were cool like that an' we always talked. Not once wit him was I gon' say somethin', but stopped 'cause I was gon' bey somethin', which really meant I was gon' slay somethin'.

Yeah, I see only some of y'all followed me there. Unlike my boys, who don't appreciate my flair.

I know. It's not my fault my boys think I'm bougie. It's not my fault my moms didn't want me to be cut down by Uzis with bullets in my throat and my spine and my intestines and my mind and my lungs and my heart while playing ball at the park until it's no streetlights and it's dark, so my mother and Michael thought it better if we cycle on the North Shore for survival because stray bullets aren't choosy so they made a decision while boozy and bought a mansion from Suzy with an in-floor Jacuzzi and a waterfall of a doozy and Chef Fabien the foodie and six bedrooms and six bathrooms that are all kinds of roomy, but the three-car garage that's heated is just looney.

I can dig it, though.

My moms and stepfather wanted to give their children a life with no ammo, but all impresario. So they told me, Jade, Jordan, Jocelyn, and Michaela it was time for some paella at a North Shore gala and then on to Venezuela to smoke a panatela.

They even handed us a cigar each, though Michael went full asshole and tried to hold it up out of Michaela's reach. He probably thought she would throw a fit and screech, but he didn't know she had mad hops from working out on the beach.

Y'all, none of us smoked that cigarillo (yeah, shows you how much I know). But if they told us they bought a wide-brimmed chapeau from some five and dime in Fargo that came with a backhoe to move mountains of snow, then we still wouldn't know how much dough went into that weird as hell cigar show.

So, they tried to explain in synchronized voices not at all strained that they didn't want their porch bloodstained or their favorite Black boy detained. That I understood. It was my scenario, in all likelihood.

But Mama and Michael wouldn't let me be felled by that blow.

So, they used their cash flow to buy a bougie-ass chateau in the North Shore suburb of Glencoe and escape the kilos of coco for our own private Idaho. Complete with an Italian grotto and three acres of well-manicured meadow.

But my boys don't understand that. They probably think I should demand that my family return stat to the South Side and The Manor where our friendships began at.

Yeah right. As if I'm the man, Jack (I think in my Richard Pryor voice), and I want to hang back (as if I really have a choice).

But it's cool.

I can't fault my boys for getting on me about my intelligence and my school. I mean, every single day Black people come into some money (or don't) and go full on bougie fool (I won't), buying McMansions furnished with red carpet stanchions to protect their semi-precious jewels from thoughts of forty acres and a mule.

Not that Mama or Michael adhere to those hard and fast bougie rules. But they're getting there. They've stuck their big toes in the wading pool.

(Next week, they interview RecSoc planners to get recommendations for Jocelyn on the best riding schools and manners.)

"I bet he got him a white girl."

Pretty Boy Blue look down the street as if his words complete an incantation so offbeat it would only summon the beautiful an' the sweet: my girl Kee-Kee to join us in this midsummer heat. I hope his ghettospell is weak, 'cause right now I really don't want to hear her speak.

I know that's wrong, but it juss gon' be a prolonged argument 'bout how I act like my shit don't stink. I know it do, but that ain't what she think I think.

"Yo."

One by one, I look at my boys, darin' any one of them to interrupt me.

"Why y'all talkin' 'bout me as if I ain't here?"

The kickoff of this one-sided dick off is startin' to bug me.

"Y'all got somethin' to say to me, say it."

It's been a minute, but my boys should know they can still trus' me. I mean, if they really want, all they have to do is suss me.

"Y'all got somethin' to ax me, ax it."

An' they should know I ain't gon' get mad if they cuss me.

"So is this gon' be the last time we ever see you?"

E's look dares me to flee. I swear, no matter what I say, he gon' flat out judge me.

"'Cause Ms. Edna Mae turn seventy-five juss once."

How I really want to answer is, "E, my ace boon coon since Covey One and Ms. McMahon's homeroom, please don't begrudge me."

"An' it ain't like you got no other reason to come to the Wild Hunneds."

Man. This new look on his face. Yeah, he's already misjudged me.

I lift my chin at the Conquest Knight XV. Y'all, this bad bitch is beastly.

"My moms an' stepfather didn't drop buckets of ducats on that fo' nothin'."

It was made in Canada, juss like Jason Priestley.

"They knew they was gon' be comin' to the Wild Hunneds e'ry now an' then to visit Ms. Edna Mae."

My moms an' stepfather bought it wit a big splash of cash an' said to hell wit a lease fee. Nah, the two of them don't do nothin' cheaply.

Especially when they go see me in Fiji test-fly a top secret exo-suit while speaking Swahili. And then do the same thing in Tahiti—all on the down low and State of Illinois ROTC sneaky.

(Y'all don't know this, but an entire family can get top secret clearance when your parents have so much money it's misconstrued as superior brilliance.)

"Do what you need to do, nwafa, but juss know she be axin' 'bout you." Nate says that as if I'm done wit The Manor an' this is my last appearance.

"Yeah, man. She think you got a white girl 'cause you ain't respond to none of her TruTells since y'all left." Pretty Boy Blue say that as if I all but said to my girl is "good riddance."

"Don't trip. White girls can suck a mean dick." Typical Big Sherm. Pullin' shit out of left field to justify his entire existence.

"Nwafa, yo' mama can suck a mean dick, but don't ax me how I know."

The fuck? Since when did I say bogus-ass shit like a motherfucking schmuck?

Don't nobody say nothin' fo' 'bout a minute. My boys are as surprised as I am that I just went and put my foot all up in it. Talking about how each other's mamas try to conversate wit the dirty llama has always been off limits.

So, I'm not quite sure how the fuck I just did it. Pissed off my boys, I mean, so bad they gon' picket. Yeah, from them I don't need to hear it. I know I've been a supreme asshole and motherfuckin' idjit.

Just take a look at what my dumbassery elicits. It's on ag'in like a surfboard an' Gidget.

Big Sherm lands a soft straight right jab on my chin, but I take it like smallpox took the borough of Brooklyn and that swordsman took the swarthy head of Anne Boleyn. I counter feint with an Ali Shuffle left and an Ali Shuffle right before I unleash a vicious left uppercut with all my blustering might.

To be honest, I'm surprised Big Sherm doesn't take flight (*bang! zoom!* straight to the Moon), even though that fluffy swing can bring the impotent power only a nonexistent Category Five hurricane would sling.

Y'all, my fist alights upon Big Sherm's chin as softly as a sprite, an' e'rybody is surprised it's this wispy haymaker scrunch punch that ends the whole goddamn fight. Big Sherm don't know it yet, but it's time for him to tell Ms. Irene good night.

I send him rumblin', stumblin', an' bumblin' onto his big ass where he scatters twigs an' grass. But my overweight pugilistic mate refuses to lose an' admit his chin made of glass.

Instead, he struggles to his knees, but can't see the forest for the trees—or find his mouthpiece while wearing skis. Yeah, this is Mike Tyson making cheese in front of hundreds and hundreds of Japanese after Buster Douglas just knocked him out with (seemingly) the greatest of ease.

And just so y'all know, I admit that with some unease, but I for damn sure won't say Buster Douglas threw his punches with any sort of technical expertise.

Nate drops to his knees an' give Big Sherm a ten count as he wheeze. But when Big Sherm finally stands, it's too late an' Nate wave his hands, puts his arms 'round Big Sherm to make sure he understand, an' then raise my arm to declare me champion of The Manor, Slag Valley, an' all the South Deering land.

"Yo."

This time, I duck my head so I can't look my boys in the eye. Juss like I did the day I was leavin' 'cause I was damn sure 'bout to cry. I didn't, but that don't mean my eyes couldn't be hidden.

"I'm sorry. I went too far wit that one." My apology for my boys comes unbidden.

"Too far?" Big Sherm make a face like he juss walked in the kitchen an' his mama cookin' chitlins.

"Nwafa, yo' dumbass didn't juss go too far. You done drove off the end of the pier." Nate also got a face, but his look like he sittin' on the toilet shittin'.

"I bet that's how them white boys do up in Bougieland." Pretty

Boy Blue ain't got the stank face, but I can tell in his tone (an' his word choice) he don't give a damn at all 'bout that northern suburban white space.

I have a feeling that what I'm about to unpack from this metaphorical suitcase will have my boys questioning my birthplace and me wondering if I'm just a test case. But yet, I push on like astronaut King Kong out into deep space.

"Y'all won't believe how them white boys do yo' mama jokes up there."

There's a part of me (somewhere in this headspace) that absolutely must show my boys what's lackin' in their white people knowledge base.

"Them motherfuckers say some cruel-ass shit."

But now as I try to do that, all I can see is me in a blue hat driving away from The Manor with nothing but a gotdamn cool point disgrace.

"It threw me at first. I was like, what the fuck? Who the fuck are these assholes?"

So instead, I play the role, front like my ego just got swole, even though my awkwardness has definitely put me in my place.

"But I caught on quick. I had to make sure I kept up wit them white boys an' held my own."

But that doesn't mean I can't have fun as I tell this story as part of my Raf's Chopp'd an' Screw'd Comedy Showcase.

"Man, them white boys ain't seen a yo' mama joke they don't like. The more offensive, the better."

But my boys are looking at me as if I'm in the process of rebooking my flee back to my bougie disgrace.

"So I brought it an' then some. E'ry. Damn. Day."

That line was supposed to be strong, like the United States in the 1980s and the Cold War arms race.

"An' that's the problem. I'm used to bringin' the heat like that on a regular basis, so I guess I juss got caught up in the moment."

Instead, it don't got no chill and registers nil, like set to zero, which engenders Euclidean flat space.

"Tole y'all Raf was turnin' white."

Speakin' of no chill, it's about time for me to go die on a hill, 'cause what Pretty Boy Blue juss said was ill.

"Black on the outside. White on the inside. Straight up Oreo."

But then Nate gotta go an' get all up in my grill.

"Double Stuff Oreo."

And Big Sherm start lickin' his lips like he 'bout to go get his fill. Where, I don't know, but it's lookin' less likely I'm gon' have to die on this hill.

"Nwafa, you juss wanna get yo' grub on."

See, E is blessed when he says shit like this in jest. He's always known to squash the noise between me and my boys. More than once, he has saved us all from the oncoming squall of a nasty and permanent friendship downfall.

I give E a slight but grateful nod for deflectin' these attacks an' awful prods, but I make sure I keep a straight face so I don't tip off the rest of our squad.

"You goddamn right. Ain't no shame in my inhale game."

Big Sherm pats his big belly (which fondly remembers Welch's grape jelly), remindin' us all again he could be the Black avatar of the philosopher he thinks was born in Delhi. Or how he think Tupac is the real Machiavelli.

"This motherfucker need to go wit Raf an' 'em back to Bougieland so he can eat up all they cows an' pigs an' horses an' chickens an' shit in that castle they got."

Nate don't know the half of it. Nah, he wouldn't even be able to do the math of it. If Big Sherm came home wit us, multiple nuts would be bust once he saw how our enormous refrigerator an' freezer was stocked an' stuffed.

"Y'all 'member when I ate forty-two chicken wings at that block party when we was eight years old?"

Big Sherm say that like he proud an' extremely chuffed.

"Nwafa, of course we 'member—"

"—yo' motherfuckin' ass had so much chicken grease—"

"—all over yo' mouth—"

"—yo' mama wiped it off, put it in a plastic container—"

"—an' then put that in the freezer until winter—"

"—so she could use it to moisturize yo' dry ass, cracked up, ashy-ass lips—"

"—an' when winter came an' yo' mama put that chicken grease on yo' lips, Kee-Kee—"

Nate starts jumpin' up and down because saying my ex-girl's name lays that TruTell electricity all the way down and brings four times the disapproving frowns.

"TruTell, disable the Kee-Kee Protocol." That's E initiating the closedown.

"I thought we needed majority assent to do that."

"We do."

"But Reese isn't here."

"Reese don't got to be here."

"Yeah, he done already gave his approval."

"When the fuck did that happen?"

"When you was fuckin' eatin' caviar in Bougieland."

"That's not fair. I didn't ask my parents to move me to the suburbs."

"We all know you like it there better than you like it here."

"How do you kn—"

"When was the last time you looked at the Protocol?"

"The day he left the Manor."

"The last time we saw him."

"The last time Kee-Kee saw him."

"Yo, I been busy an' shit tryin' to—"

"—make sure you don't talk like that 'round all them white people?"

"What?"

"Look, man, ain't nobody tryin' to get no seizures juss 'cause you—"

"—ashamed to have Kee-Kee—"

"—sussed by them white people up in Bougieland—"

"—so you ain't gon' think about her—"

"—dream about her—"

"—or TruTell about her—"

"—wit them white people—"

"—us—"

"—or anybody fuckin' else."

"It's completely fuckin' obvious you straight wiped her entirely out of yo' life."

"Which means you pro'lly don't e'en know she be axin' 'bout you—"

"—'cause you pro'lly set up auto delete for all TruTell comms from her—"

"—so she be axin' us—"

"—when you comin' through next—"

"—or tellin' us—"

"—to tell you stuff—"

"—but ain't none of us tryin' to twitch out—"

"—wit no motherfuckin' dampenin' enhancements—"

"—so yeah, fuck a Kee-Kee Protocol."

"I'm not ashamed of her."

"Then TruTell her that."

"Nah, let's start wit us first, since—"

"—we 'posed to be yo' boys an' all, so—"

"—turn yo' damn SussShare back on—"

"—so we know how you really feel 'bout us—"

"—'cause ain't that why our mamas voted to let Stanford Sutton Industries—"

"—put this shit—"

"—inside us? I mean—"

"—well, I really did it fo' the scratch, 'cause—"

"—you scratch my back an' pay my mama's rent fo' life—"

"—an' I scratch yo' back an' give you unfettered permission to invade my privacy fo' life—"

"—so activate that shit again so we can know if we still yo' boys or not."

For the second time today, don't nobody say shit. It's as if we all can't move as we watch the embodiment of laryngitis hit. I swear, for the first time in my life, I feel like I'm 'bout to have a fit.

I'm talm 'bout so apoplectic that I'm gon' start speakin' in tongues, includin' Sanskrit. But then Big Sherm's older brother rolls up on us in his electric blue Honda Transmitt an' stops on the street in front of Ms. Edna Mae's house where the curb is split.

He don't get out the car 'cause the Transmitt can let him talk to people from afar by usin' a holographic image of him as Jafar.

"Bring ya ass. Jamaal was playin' ball at Trumbull Park an' got popped."

I think it's bizarre that people who live in such poverty spend money on shit they can't afford like they just won the lottery.

"Some fools rolled up on the courts in a matte black Nova, an' we know who be ridin' an' glidin' in that. That nwafa D Scone."

It's almost as if they're inexorably drawn to the worst sort of gaudery.

"J was hit four times. I sussed e'erbody else."

Yeah, I know. That's just my North Shore snobbery.

"Let's be up."

So I should stop this sidity mockery. And I do.

Before E gets in the Transmitt, he turns and lifts his chin to me. I lift my chin back at him to say goodbye properly.

I want to actually say something to him. But I just sit there on Ms. Edna Mae's porch, because my world is about to go dim. I'm certain this will be the last time he and I are in the limn. And yeah, I know; that is fucking grim.

I'm still sitting here when they *skurr!!!* away from the curb. I promise y'all, though; I'm not perturbed.

I'm just trying not to cry.

But I do.

No sound. No shakes. Pre-grief come true.

After about fifteen minutes, a voice behind me speaks, as if in a Black Hand Side clinic. She's not sure if my tears have reached their limit.

I don't say this, because I'm damn sure I already convey this, but yeah, the salty runoff has diminished. Right now, at this very moment, I'm finished.

I don't wipe my face before I turn to see who it is, because, between you, me, and her, she already up in my biz. I bet she can tell me exactly what just happened, if I gave her a pop quiz.

But no need to go that route. My boys clued her in, no doubt.

She sits down and I frown at the red digital countdown beneath the skin around her neck. I'm shocked, y'all; an Electric Resurrected Kee-Kee is something I didn't expect. I'm not sure her showing me this, though, has the desired effect.

"Why?" I ask her.

She puts her soft, small palms on my face and slides them down to wipe the tears away. I have somewhat of an idea about what she's going to say.

"Not all of us have a rich mama and step daddy to move us out of The Manor."

True. But does that mean this was the only thing left for her to do?

"Stanford Sutton Institute?"

"No. Virginia. Women's basketball in The Forty-Eight isn't

suspicious and afraid of the Electric Resurrected, like how football is. Like how you are."

That's a low blow, if I ever felt it. It's even worse, because she dealt it. "I'm not afraid."

"Then prove it. Stanford Sutton said if I convince you to undergo Electric Resurrection, then he'll give me an extra 8,760 hours of battery life. A redshirt year."

That motherfucker. Yeah, no pressure. Right now, he's probably smiling wide and bright, full-on Cheshire.

"Do you believe him?"

"Why wouldn't I? Two months ago, my mama and I signed my Electric Resurrection contract. The redshirt hours clause is in it, along with my official brand name: Nyanza Swift. The next extremely fast Electric Resurrection point guards—second gen, third gen, fourth gen, whatever gen—will wear my brand and have my face."

Holy shit. Sounds like her mama bargained with only one thought to wit: a brand spankin' new one-of-a-kind identi-kit.

"So, you not mad at me?"

"Watchu think, nwafa?"

Kee-Kee smirks at me, and I want her to stroll down green tea aisles with me.

"You lucky we movin' next door to y'all next week. You also lucky me holdin' a grudge against you will shorten my battery life due to the vitriol. I'm not about to live less minutes and hours because of you. I'm trying to live my life in numeric digital red, for as long as I can."

I got that covered.

I smile and throw my arm around her neck, kiss the countdown charm around her neck, and spread some lip smarm around her neck.

"I'm sorry."

"Damn right you are. On more than one level."

I don't dispute that. She came correct; I don't need to compute that.

"You know how you can make it up to me, don't you?"

"Already on it. Just sent Stanford Sutton an InTell and told him I'm down for Electric Resurrection. Told him I'm doing it for you. Also, made a demand: 8,760 free redshirt hours for me, and if he agrees, you and I will be his first-gen spokesmodels."

She raises an eyebrow at me. She's pro'lly wonderin' if she wants to be this highbrow wit me.

"It's cool. I've thought it through. We're going to lead the Electric Resurrection Athletes Squad (yeah, I made it up; we're superheroes). We'll tour college campuses in The Forty-Eight and show them that Electric Resurrected athletes aren't overpowered and dangerous. Stanford Sutton's pockets will get fatter, and because he'll forever need us, we'll live long Electric Resurrected lives."

Kee-Kee twists her mouth to one side. Yeah, she's still pissed off at me. I bet if she could, she'd twist off my feet.

"Superheroes? Nwafa, you think you slick. This is what you were diabolically devising instead of answering my TruTells, right?"

"Partly."

"And the other part?"

"Being an asshole to you."

"At least you know what you are."

"I think we all need to connect with our inner being every now and then."

"Not like that."

"I know. Again, I'm sorry."

"Is that what happens when you move to the North Shore?"

I want to tell her yes, and be definitive, but that's such a loaded question, and she'll misconstrue my indicative.

So, instead I say:

"Let me know in a week."

INTRO. ALL I'M EVER GON' DO IS STAY BLACK AND DIE JEAN-MICHEL FEAT. KINSLEY CHASE

1. RAINBOWS AN' KANGOLS JEAN-MICHEL FEAT. THE JOURNO CREW

2. ONE HUNDRED PERCENT PERFORMANCE OUTPUT JEAN-MICHEL FEAT. KINSLEY CHASE

3. IN THE TRUTELL EMO JEAN-MICHEL FEAT. MICHAËLLE-ANNABELLE

4. YOUR BCID MUST HAVE REACHED ITS UPLOAD LIMIT FEAT. JEAN-MICHEL AND SAFFRON SUTTON

INTERLUDE. THIS IS YOUR (FAKE) LIFE SAFFRON SUTTON

5. KAI-KA SHON-SHON

6. ME, THAT LOVEABLE, CUDDLY, FUZZY BLACK RABBIT JEAN-MICHEL FEAT. KINSLEY CHASE

7. A SWEET-ASS HELICOPTER AND TEN STATER STRANGERS? JEAN-MICHEL FEAT. THE NAUGHTY NINETY-DAY FANDANGO

8. I DO EXPERIENCE THE TRAUMATIC JEAN-MICHEL FEAT. SAFFRON SUTTON'S PATH THUGS

9. IN THE TRUTELL (PART ONE) MICHAËLLE-ANNABELLE

10. IN THE TRUTELL (PART TWO) JEAN-MICHEL FEAT. ESMÉE VÉRITÉ

11. POST-ELECTRIC RESURRECTION JEAN-MICHEL FEAT. SAFFRON SUTTON

INTERLUDE. JEAN-MICHEL AND THE BUGATTI CHIRON SUPER SPORT 300+ EXO-SUIT THAT LOVES HIM

12. THIS IS THE TRUTELL MICHAËLLE-ANNABELLE FEAT. JEAN-MICHEL

13. A HIDDEN MEMORY, AS ABRASIVE AS EMERY JEAN-MICHEL FEAT. KINSLEY CHASE

14. A COLLOQUY. MICHAËLLE-ANNABELLE AND SAFFRON SUTTON

15. AN UNLIKELY ALLIANCE FORGED RAKAYA'S LURKSUIT FEAT. RAKAYA, BIG MAMA BLACK, AND ROSHAN

16. STANFORD SUTTON AND THE NCAA AIN'T STRONGER THAN OUR LOVE LOVE? ESMÉE VÉRITÉ FEAT. JEAN-MICHEL, TUSKEGEE NORTH ACE EXO-SUIT PILOT

OUTRO. YOUNG, RESURRECTED AND BLACK JEAN-MICHEL

Code Switching

INTRO. ALL I'M EVER GON' DO IS
STAY BLACK AND DIE
JEAN-MICHEL FEAT. KINSLEY CHASE

Kinsley Chase sits on manman mwen plastic-covered couch. The InTell HumbleBrag subprogram Stanford Sutton Industries chipped me with says she's wearing a circa 2020 Theresa Frostad Eggesbø Resurrection skinload.

I had no idea this shit actually worked. I don't HumbleBrag. I thought it was all about narcissism and went in one direction, so I said fuck that shit.

But Kinsley Chase HumbleBraggin' 'bout how unique (meanin' how expensive) her skinload is makes sense. These days, pourin' honey like that into some poor Black people's ear can be an effective war propaganda tool. We all know both the State of Illinois and the Sovereign State of Chicago recruitin'.

Too bad I don't like siwo. Or lagè.

'Sides, manman mwen and I don't need no tools. We juss need to pay our bills.

I don't sit up from the couch across from Kinsley Chase. I don't think I could sit up if I wanted to. And not just because the sweat on my cheek has fused it to the plastic. I'm close. It's about my time.

Mwen toujou wè li just fine from this position. She's got this chin-length dirty blonde straight razor cut. Eyes I can't tell whether they're blue or gray. Full (for a white girl) Cupid's bow lips. The skin of a rich, twenty-two-year-old white girl expat who lives in Corfu.

And just so y'all know, she ain't all that. I see all this 'cause I can't look nowhere else or turn over the other way. I need to conserve my energy for the press conference tomorrow.

She puts her palms under her chin to frame her face and smiles at me. "We do good work, don't we?"

I nod. Reluctantly. "What do you really look like?" This ain't the first skinload I've seen her wear.

She turns a bit sideways to pose so I can see her profile. "What do you think I really look like?"

I smirk. "Maybe like that. I mean, you might be Norwegian for real, but I have a hard time believing the bullshit your HumbleBrag is tellin' me."

She gives me a wry smile. "And why is that?"

I kiss my teeth. *Tchuip.* "I can't even remember how long ago it was when y'all said y'all was gon' Electric Resurrect me, but here I am. Still alive. Still dyin'."

"We're true to our word. *I'm* true to my word. Remember, I am a Tenth Degree Maven. I cannot lie."

Tchuip. "Nah, see, you ain't slick. I know how your SPark Creed goes, an' it ain't the way you juss said it. You tryin' to be cute wit yo' words. It's 'posed to go: 'I, Kinsley Chase, am true to my word and my profession. As a Tenth Degree Maven, I cannot lie in a manner that brings harm and detriment to the company or organization that bought and currently holds my PR Guild contract.'"

She laughs. It's the same one I've heard before. That's the only real thing about her.

"The first time I met your mother," she says, "she looked me up and down and then told me: 'I don' brook no fools.' I take it you don't, either."

Tchuip. Louder this time. "Yeah, that's you in there for real. No matter what skinload you wear, you still talk and move like a white girl."

She gives me a tiny smile. I can't read it, and it's not because of the way I'm lying on the couch.

Kinsley Chase stands. "Make sure you arrive an hour early for the press conference tomorrow."

I scowl at her. "Not all Black people run on CP time."

"I didn't say you or all Black people do."

I struggle to sit up, and not because the plastic sucks at my cheek, trying to keep me down. "Ki fè la a, what are you trying to say?"

"Familiarize yourself with the Bugatti Chiron Super Sport 300+ exo-suit specs I just sent you."

Her tiny smile is gone. And then, so is she.

Shit just got real. And I don't know why.

1. RAINBOWS AN' KANGOLS
JEAN-MICHEL FEAT. THE JOURNO CREW

I don't make eye contact with no one. I ain't here for fun. I juss pull my orange an' blue Walter Payton College Prep hood low over my face. Yeah, I'm tryin' to ghost this space. Post haste. I'm gon' start this race; y'all do y'all's part an' be sure to give me chase. 'Cause y'all know y'all will. Anything for a story.

My story. His story. All glory.

But not for a DuSable Haitian lookin' to find a place in those rich suburban tech spaces.

I juss want my life extended. Amended an' splendid. Open-ended an' uncontended. A chance to share they world an' truly be in it.

But they won't even let me smell the North Shore peonies as I lie in a meadow there waitin' for the dark of night an' the risin' of the Pleiades while I think of my girl Esmée Vérité. If I tried all that, they'd tell me, "Nwafa, please go back to your monkey trees because we know you can't afford Stanford Sutton's android fees." And they'd say it to my face, but wit a smirk an' civil ease.

So here we are. Me looking through the bell jar at these reporters who crossed sovereign state borders so I could be drawn and quartered—

Nah, these ain't my ace boon coon Chicago reporters. These are them Stater journos wishin' this press conference wit me was a circle-jerk holo-vid porno.

Yeah, I said it. That's what they do. Them grafs they gon' write about me tonight won't be nothin' new. It's gon' be the same ol' same ol', but not rainbows an' Kangols.

(Electric blue. Coolin'. Stylin'. Sharp.)

My e'ry movement gon' be chronicled by these Stater journos whose dislike of me is so comical they should be wearin' tweed an' squintin' through monocles. White men is all I see (except for this one white girl in front of me who looks like her name should be Brie). They gon' describe me at this presser in exquisite detail, includin' my hoodie an' how I never failed to exhale in frustration when I kissed my teeth in disbelief at they questions.

Tchuip.

An' that's juss for starters.

Oh my stars an' garters, these white men gon' holler—high-pitched an' shrill, as if they goin' over a cliff in a car like Mr. Bill—that I slouched into the press conference late; sauntered up to the dais wit an exaggerated pimp gait, stared at the floor when I answered they questions, scratched my chin 'cause I was bored of they questions, sulked in my hood 'cause I was too good for they questions, curled my lip when I ignored they quips—

Yeah, this gon' be a trip.

But I'm prepared to be berated an' castigated as if I ejaculated on the hood of the Stater governor's black Mercedes an' then smacked a Stater baby. Nah, these Stater journos ain't sympathetic to a seventeen-year-old diabetic whose kidney failure ain't respected 'cause they don't think he should have ever been considered for the Resurrected Electric.

Now, y'all watch as this press conference gets hectic.

"Do you think it's fair that the NCAA denied your petition to play football at Auburn University?"

"No."

"Are you going to submit an appeal to the NCAA Committee on Competitive Safeguards and Medical Aspects of Sports?"

"No."

"But you're dying. Your doctor said you only have weeks to live."

"Still no."

Electric Resurrection. Born again perfection. The six-zero correction.

That's what them rich ass State of Illinois livin', keepin' up with the Joneses driven, buyin' the mansions of Jeremy Piven—

(Does he still live in the North Shore? Is he even alive anymore? I loved him in *Smokin' Aces* wit Common, plus Alicia an' Taraji's pretty faces.)

—white kids call it. Wit no thought about the wallet. Status is the only thing that matters to these State of Illinois crackers.

Y'all should see them white kids up there draftin' an' craftin' a *Stand by Me* lardass mass of post-suicide instructions (wit no reluctance) for they parents to commission Stanford Sutton Industries to build a perfect body (no contrition) designed pre-suicide (wit careful ambition) by spoiled teenagers who all day wishin' they nose or they lips or they tits or they dicks was a very different vision.

But when my Black ass tried to ask for the six zeroes? I got three rows of assholes tellin' me them bungalows on my street in Chicago was too shabby to be held up solo against they Stater investment portfolios. Nah, it don't matter that I'm from the Sovereign State of Tomorrow, better known as Chicago. Them Staters ain't got no sorrow for a poor Black boy who can't find two buttons to borrow.

(Yeah, I don't know what it mean, neither; when Manman speak, I juss believe her.)

"Chris Robertson with *The New City Republican* here. You were born and raised in Chicago. The South Side. Jeffrey Manor. Rough and tumble urban jungle. Your father is a deadbeat dad. Your mother is poor. Dirt poor. We're talking having-trouble-scraping-together-coin-for-the-guild-coffers poor, and that's with the Maids, Cleaners, and Launderers Guild having one of the lowest—if not the lowest—guild dues in your city-state. Your mother doesn't have Electric Resurrection money, and yet, you're turning down a full-ride scholarship and the chance at extended life. Shouldn't you appeal?"

"No."

Kounye a, make sure y'all hear me on this, as if I'm a trumpet bein' played by Wynton Marsalis. See that Stater journo three rows back? Yeah, him over there who was juss talkin' smack. He keep on runnin' his mouth like that 'bout manman mwen as if she lesser an' I for damn sure ain't gon' behave up in this presser.

W te tande m. Yeah, y'all heard me. I didn't stutter. I ain't scared of this journo horde, B; that's my mother.

I'm gon' start breakin' shit up in here (lights, cameras, crackers) if that journo don't catch some fear an' realize that's manman mwen an' I cherish madanm sa somethin' dear.

"Trevor Atkins with *The Hilltop Examiner* here. How much did Stanford Sutton Industries quote you for your Electric Resurrection?"

"I don't know."

"You don't know?"

"No."

"How do you not know this? This is literally life and death we're talking about here. Stanford Sutton Industries must have quoted your mother and Auburn University a price. Stanford Sutton Industries must have dragged some nice, big, fat round number across the holo-table for your mother. Gynoids, androids, and paedroids don't grow on trees. Those are expensive and exclusive products, especially the paedroids. They can't be paid for with hopes and dreams. Stanford Sutton Industries doesn't conduct financial transactions with Monopoly money."

Tand 'on koze. Listen to this bullshit. M pa sezi. But I ain't surprised. Not one bit.

These djèdjè don't think I'm worthy 'cause my skin too dirty. Se dakò. Non, really, it's all right; I still love Mica-Mireille Arceneaux, who birthed me.

She ain't gon' be happy, though, when she read them Stater stories tomorrow. I'm gon' tell manman mwen to gorge on that Chicago holo-news feed first, an' then pick at that Stater low-fat junk slow, best to worst, preppin' my wince face for when she cuss. 'Cause y'all know she will.

(But don't worry; manman mwen still gon' be at church on Sunday mornin', bright an' early.)

"Jim Becker with *The North Shore Clarion*. Did Stanford Sutton Industries give you a date for resurrection?"

"Yes."

"So, when is it?"

"That ain't none of y'all's business."

"Listen, son. Do you really want that to be your response?"

"Wi. Especially since I ain't gon' go through wit it. Next question."

"Brett Larsen here. In five minutes, the *Patriot-Whig Standard* will break the news that you're a selfish, ungrateful son who doesn't love his mother because she kicked out of the house the only person you've ever loved in this world—your father—when you were five years old, and your decision to not appeal the NCAA's ruling is your way of getting back at her for that. Twelve years later. I want to give you a chance to respond to this on the record before this news breaks and everyone in your city-state and everyone in the North Shore is talking about it. What do you have to say to that?"

"Ala de kaka."

"I don't know what—"

"It means that's bullshit."

"Fine. Call it what you will. My feature will also mention the secret deal your mother has just made with Stanford Sutton Industries, which, in part, states that she will go into cryo-sleep at their labs, allowing Stanford Sutton's scientists to conduct all the research and experiments on her they want, as long as Stanford Sutton Industries first: waive all Electric Resurrection fees in the contract your mother signed months ago; second, include a new clause to re-up you every year after the first five years of your Electric Resurrection, which will last the duration of your natural lifespan—as long as the cryo research on your mother yields satisfactory results; and third, waive any and all fees associated with Auburn University regarding your Electric Resurrection. What do you say to that?"

"For the bilingually challenged like Mesye Larsen here: That's also bullshit."

"You really want that to be your quote?"

"Next question."

"The *Standard* is not the only outlet that can break news. Jack Carlson from the *Beacon Hill Banner* here. My sources tell me that, considering the large amount of money Auburn University has invested in you, the Committee will allow you to play this fall, but only if you agree to Stanford Sutton Industries reducing your performance output to forty percent. What do you have to say to that?"

"Next question."

"Ray Malone, freelance holo-vid journalist extraordinaire here. Some people believe that, for a person—a human—to truly experience emotions, you must have a flesh-and-blood heart and you must have a wrinkled, grey matter brain. You have those right now, but I also notice you look upset and disappointed. Are you refusing Electric Resurrection because you won't have a flesh-and-blood heart, you won't have a wrinkled, grey matter brain, and you're afraid you will no longer have true human emotions?"

"Next question."

"Are you afraid you won't feel like yourself, if you undergo Electric Resurrection?"

"Next question."

"Are you afraid you won't feel like a real boy?"

"Next question."

"Danny Meyer here from *The New Times Republican*. I'm not sure where Malone is getting his information, but it's been proven that, if one were to undergo Electric Resurrection, one would feel like a real boy or girl. Scores of teenagers in the North Shore undergo the procedure every day, and they keep whatever memories they want intact. These teenagers have programming that is very complex, sophisticated, and detailed. They emote. They have feelings.

"That is the crux of this NCAA rumor we keep hearing about, Jean-Michel: You will not be allowed to practice or play after you undergo Electric Resurrection unless your performance output is reduced to forty percent because the Committee is concerned you will retain the anger we see in you now—which we've also seen in you this past year since you've become terminally ill—and unleash it without mercy upon your opponents on the football field. Is that your concern as well?"

"W'ap pale pawòl tafya. Nah, it's cool; I know you don't understand, so I'll say it in plain English: That's some straight crazy nonsense. Y'all actin' like I'm the Incredible Hulk or Wolverine or somebody. As if I got some volatile, dangerous anger pent up in me that I can't control."

"Kristin Mueller here from *The Drumheller Post*. But Jean-Michel, be honest with us: That *is* what you're worried about, isn't it? That is why you won't undergo Electric Resurrection. As an athlete, a football player, you realize how dangerous Electric Resurrection can be on the field, for both your teammates and your opponents. That's why you're declining Stanford Sutton's offer, right?"

"Next question."

"OK then, do you agree with the NCAA's ruling?"

"No."

"The NCAA is concerned that you will be much faster after Electric Resurrection. What do you think?"

"I won't."

"The NCAA is also concerned that you will be much stronger after Electric Resurrection. What do you think?"

"I won't."

"How do we know you won't?"

"Stanford Sutton Industries assured me that the programmin' his coders would give my electric resurrected body would be the exact same speed an' strength as I was on my last day of full health. They didn't tell me nothin' 'bout no forty percent output performance. So, if I was to undergo Electric Resurrection, there won't be nothin' dangerous 'bout it an' there won't be nothin' dangerous 'bout me."

"But how do we know that? How do we know we can trust the programming?"

"Y'all juss bragged 'bout how them teenagers in the North Shore—"

"But, as one of my colleagues just said, it's been proven that Stanford Sutton Industries can capture a deceased person's memories whole, intact, and accurately, and transfer those memories to the resurrected body they've built, which results in true, believable human feelings. On the other hand, Electric Resurrection for athletes—especially ones like you who come from places like you do—includes memories, feelings, and experiences that have not been proven yet to engender a safe performance output. The NCAA just doesn't know what your Electric Resurrected body will do on the field with your experiences and memories inside it. So, from a legal perspective, they can only risk this with a significant performance output reduction.

"But you say none of this is a concern for you. So, tell us: Why won't you undergo the most coveted and expensive cosmetic procedure man has ever known, which grants you veritable immortality, with no money coming out of your mother's pocket? Kids in the North Shore literally dream about this every night, but you're thumbing your nose at it."

"How 'bout you tell the NCAA I said to let me undergo Electric Resurrection wit full performance output an' kite m montre ou there ain't nothin' to worry 'bout."

"Why don't you tell them yourself?"

"Tell them I said kite m montre ou before the season starts. Kite m montre ou on practice holo-vid."

"Look, the NCAA is reluctant to take its first chance at a sports-based Electric Resurrection on you because—"

"I'm Black. An' DuSable Haitian."

"No, because you'd be dangerous on the field."

"Non, what you really mean is me bein' Black an' DuSable Haitian makes me dangerous on the field, eske se pa sa?"

"Don't put words in my mouth. What I really mean is you want me to tell the NCAA to let you give them a workout once you undergo Electric Resurrection, but how do I, how do we—how do they—know you won't just go half-speed? How do they know you won't just play down your augmented speed and strength during the workout, and then unleash it on the field when the season starts?"

"Y'all really like that word unleash. It's a perfect one to put on young Black boys who make the same tackles an' same blocks as them white boys in the North Shore. When they do it, y'all write, 'Hayden Keliher, All-State left tackle and National Honor Society member, cleaned the Sam linebacker's clock to open a hole for his tailback, who scored the game-winning touchdown on fourth and goal.'

"But when we do it, y'all write, 'Siméon Andrevil, juvenile delinquent an' despicable Ro Boy gang member, unleashed violence an' fury an' mayhem on the quarterback when he sacked him on fourth and goal wit no time left on the clock to win the game.' Juss tell the NCAA te'm montre w, machè."

"Steve Schultz here. I don't know about the school districts of my fellow journalists here, but District 65 in Lake Bluff and District 115 in Lake Forest offered eight foreign languages at both the elementary and high school levels back when I got my education, and Haitian Creole wasn't one of them. I have no idea what that gobbledygook was you just mixed in with your English. But I'll say this: You could kill someone out there on the football field if you undergo Electric Resurrection. You won't be a boy. You'll be something new. Something different. Something awful and dangerous."

"*The Dispatch* agrees. Robbie Vandenberg here, by the way. Look, Jean-Michel. You won't be anything like those other kids on the field— those real kids out there—not with your upbringing, where you grew up, and how angry you are. You won't even be human. You'll be some raging, technorganic, super strong, super agile creature whose creation we all will come to regret in short order. You'll be a super-predator, no less, designed with supposed good intentions, but a monster that will eventually rip us all to pieces in the end, both literally and metaphorically. How do you feel about that?"

"Ki radòt sa? Nah, monchè, don't look at me like I juss shit in my hand an' tol' you it was chokola. Mwen serye: What kind of bullshit is that?"

Dang on. When Manman read each an' e'ery one of these Stater journos' goin'-ons at the butt-crack of tomorrow morn, mezanmi, she gon' say, "I should never have tol' you, 'Konpòte nou byen, Jean-Michel,' yesterday."

But she did. An' I couldn't. I thought about it. But I didn't.

I mean (so fresh an' so clean), why would I "be good" to these Stater journos who don't see me as nothin' but a hood? Thug is what they want to call me; I juss wish they had that Chicago journalist idolatry.

But I dig. I done went an' got too big for my britches, so now these Stater journos actin' like some punk-ass racist bitches.

I miss those Chicago sports reporters; worshippers, all of them, sussin' they internal biometric recorders toward Him. On their knees in they columns, pleadin' wit the NCAA in they columns to reverse its rulin' before autumn, juss so they can watch Him play football at Auburn.

Now, that's love.

Not like this spate of hate these Stater journos refuse to abate 'til they verbally castrate my big, Black Mandingo trouser snake so it don't gyrate wit they alabaster daughters named Kate.

(Or Madison. Or Dakota. Or Mackenzie.)

Nah, I ain't never seen nobody delight so much in somebody else's plight as these estebedje journos tonight.

"Frank Kowalski with *The New Haven Standard* here. Excuse my colleagues, Jean-Michel. They've obviously watched too many bad sci-fi B movies. I, on the other hand, have a legitimate question: How do we know your mother hasn't asked Stanford Sutton Industries to put a secret clause in that new contract, a clause that would have them program you to be an ultra robo running back?"

"Why would manman mwen do that? Why would Stanford Sutton Industries allow that?"

"Why wouldn't they? You'd win the Heisman Trophy and almost all of the other major offensive awards, take Auburn to the National Championship four years in a row and win each time, go number one in the NFL draft, and have a long, lucrative football career because you'd never get hurt. It's a win-win-win scenario for you and your mother, for Stanford Sutton Industries, and for Auburn University. So much money to be made and spent by everyone."

"Gade monchè, I wouldn't be no different than before. Tell the NCAA to let me show you that I would be the same running back as I was before the procedure. Tell them to give me a chance at full performance output."

"But how do we know you're not just looking for a chance to knock our Stater boys' heads clean off their shoulders?"

"I juss want to play ball, mesye blan. That's it. That's all. I juss want to run the rock."

2. ONE HUNDRED PERCENT PERFORMANCE OUTPUT
JEAN-MICHEL FEAT. KINSLEY CHASE

Lòske jounalis sa yo gade m—

Hold up. Let me say that again. I'll wait. Y'all go grab y'alls paper an' pen.

When these Stater journos look at me, they don't juss see a Black boy. Nah, they also see a bio-electric, battery-operated toy, part of a Stanford Sutton Industries ploy to bring fat cat football alums joy.

(Wit money. Anpil, anpil lajan.)

An' that pisses them off. So they gon' keep rushin' off an' bustin' off these queries at a machine-gun pace in my face while smirkin' at my Haitian Creole vocabulary, pretendin' they can only understand me, barely, 'cause my accent is too thick an' scary.

Pakont—but on the flip side—them Chicago reporters gon' give me the benefit of the doubt (that's right) when they write they stories witout bias tonight. They embrace a sovereign state that thrives on a black market sparked by innovation an' encouraged by a Haitian who planned a nation for secession from a State of Imperfection, then made Chicago the greatest an' said to hell wit those Stater racists.

Like the ones in front of me now.

Yeah, they got them Stater racist papers in them Stater racist places, like Rockford an' Aurora (eighty-six stories about Chicago's horrors), Joliet an' Naperville ("What's the Deal? Chicago's Black Market: Is It Real?"), Springfield an' Peoria (I never heard of ya; oh, wait, yes I have; I trounced a girl from there once named Gloria playin' holo-vid Chess-Phoria), Elgin an' Winnetka an' Champaign too (Eske nou fini? 'Cause I'm 'bout through).

So is this interview.

The gym doors bang open. In strides hope. White savior of the Black and broken. White savior from the rope.

Kinsley Chase, straight outta the North Shore, stalks in her Louboutin stiletto heels across a gym floor that features a grizzly at half-court in mid-roar.

(She wearin' this circa-2018 Charlize Theron Electric Resurrection skinload. It's been a long minute since celebrity body snatchin' been in vogue. Twenty years out of date, monchè; yeah, that Resurrection is bold. Don't tell her I said that, though, 'cause she don't want to be told. Passé or not, she still shimmerin' gold.

Short, chic blonde hair parted juss right. Makeup hardly there, but on point an' tight. Tailored two-piece Christian Dior suit bone white. Fierce face an' quick pace lettin' e'rybody know she ready to fight.)

Click, click, click, click.

(Yeah, you degoutan chen sal motherfuckers, here she come. Y'all better take flight.)

Heads turn.

(Gade lè yo, y'all djèdjè ain't bright.)

"Kristin, stop cross-examining that poor boy. Being Black doesn't make him a criminal, wrong, or an ingrate."

Click, click, click, click.

(Put yo' face to the dog, an' she gon' bite.)

Egos burn.

(Frown all you want, machè; she ain't begun to flex her might.)

"Robbie, I thought we stopped calling young Black boys super-predators more than half a century ago."

Click, click, click, click.

Internal biometric systems suss an' churn.

"Steve, fear-mongering and culture-shaming fits you like a bespoke Cole Haan suit, so I'm sure you'd be surprised to know that some of us taught ourselves how to order Prestige beer in Haitian Creole when we were sixteen years old so we could buy some during our weekend adventures to the big, bad Sovereign State."

Click, click, click, click.

Yeah, these Stater journos 'bout to learn.

"And Frank and Danny, I look forward to the countless stories you write the next few years about those white boys at New Trier and Highland Park and Glenbrook North after they undergo Electric Resurrection, where you praise them in your columns as upstanding citizens, do-gooder Eagle Scouts, and future law-abiding governors of the Land of Lincoln—even though all they'll really want to do is knock each other's heads clean off on their way to full-ride scholarships at any Division I school of their choice—where they will play at 100 percent performance output without a second thought from or restrictions imposed by the NCAA."

Kinsley sits next to me on the dais, don't even apologize for her tardy delay, but instead leans back an' waits for me to cheer hip hip hooray (nah, machè, I ain't yo' bae). When I don't say nothin', she turns to these Stater journos an' starts cussin':

"What the actual fuck, you racist motherfuckers."

The room goes dead quiet, but I know they all sussin'.

"Look at the pot calling the kettle nwafa."

That's Robbie Vandenberg, but I ain't surprised. The word nwafa ain't juss in his throat, it's even in his eyes. Yeah, this estebedje journo 'bout to win the Utmost Racist Prize.

"Monchè," I ask him, "how long you been waitin' to say 'nwafa' wit me in the same room? These last twenty minutes? Since you woke up this mornin'? From the moment your editor assigned you to this white-people-only press conference y'all juss had to have?"

Vandenberg shrugs an' smiles as if he been eatin' shit for a good long while, but yet on his plate is still a heapin' pile. "Hey, I'm just trying to get your attention. I'm just trying to help you."

This motherf—

You know what? He ain't even worth my while. But I talk shit anyway, 'cause he already done got me riled.

"Pou tout bon?" I ask, an' then spit a half-assed freestyle. "An' how you plan on doin' that? Oh, that's right, it's a notable fact: White supremacists like you live to invoke the word 'nwafa' true in the presence of a Black boy who you pray would try his damndest to come through so you can smack him down with the steel blue. And after, if the nwafa don't catch a clue? Well, it's up to you to bring the corkscrew and make sure that, for once and for all, that nwafa knows who's who. So, monchè, I know who I am, but do you know you?"

About my flow, Vandenberg don't rave. Instead, he tries to create awe wit his own personal shockwave. "Did Kinsley tell you what that Stanford Sutton Industries structure is for on Isle a la Cache?"

"No," Kinsley interrupts (her snark-shade abrupt, but her professionalism untouched), "because Kinsley is first going to tell Jean-Michel that Kinsley just got the greenlight from Stanford Sutton and the NCAA to offer Jean-Michel Electric Resurrection on Jean-Michel's terms, free of charge with no performance output reduction and no strings attached."

Silans. For three long seconds, don't nobody say a word, even though e'ry single body in this room juss heard (an' I mean that literally). Still, I ready my loins to gird (I do this skillfully) to defend against this Stater journo herd (an' score defeat brilliantly) so my big, Black Mandingo trouser snake won't be interred (by some North Shore machè named Brittany).

But I ain't scurred, especially when these Stater journos shout questions at us before they send out they suss an' make e'rybody's skin tingle wit trust. At the Medill School of Journalism, this implanted feature (biometric options an' all) is a must.

(Also known as the Lutton-Rossi device, solely created to surveil and entice, its tagline says it exposes fake news as an underhanded an' dastardly villain vice. Most of us have been duped by that kind of bullshit at least once or twice, so Medill partnered wit Stanford Sutton Industries to put that shit on ice.)

Kinsley look like she's plottin' an elaborate an' intricate diamond heist. But that's a front if I ever saw a fake bunt.

Yeah, if these Stater journos step to her wrong, she gon' unleash—

Wait. Hold up. There's that word again. Y'all juss ignore it an' go pour y'all self a gin. But if that don't calm y'all, then go ahead, unleash a feist like a three-year-old Leopold or a table flippin' Christ.

While y'all try to figure that one out, the tinglin'—

3. IN THE TRUTELL EMO
JEAN-MICHEL FEAT. MICHAËLLE-ANNABELLE

—juss stops.

It's like someone called the FCC cops or we're waitin' for the beat to drop on a track that's screwed an' chopped an' blazin' hot. The silence extends for four more seconds, handheld notifications ping wit ominous inflections, an' these Stater journos raise they voices in nonstop interjections.

"Lord Mayor Point du Sable has just declared war on the State of Illinois."

"He says the State set off a bomb at Oak Street Beach. I'm sussing reports of scores of people dead and counting."

"I'm sussing reports of possibly hundreds."

"The Mayor is calling it an act of terrorism against his beloved city-state."

"I can't fucking believe he used the word 'beloved' to describe his shitty-state."

"What the fuck is at Oak Street Beach?"

"August Twelfth fireworks."

"What the fuck is August Twelfth?"

"Some shit about Chicago being founded. Or gaining its sovereignty. Or both."

"Oak Street Beach is just one of the many locations in the city-state to hold a celebration, but it's the largest."

(These Stater journos have forgotten me)

"Now Governor Sutton has declared war on Chicago."

(so I'm 'bout to be)

"Holy shit."

"Holy shit is right. I can't independently confirm this yet with a suss, but I'm hearing Chicago is moving a significant number of heavy-plated Maybach Exelero exos to the northern and western borders."

"What about their southern border?"

"The State doesn't gives a fuck about the South Side of Chicago."

"It's not like that cesspool has the money or resources to amass an attack against us."

"Poor as shit motherfuckers."

"Speaking of shit, Atkins, you've tracked Clarabelle's cow pies all over these poor students' gymnasium floor with your Hush Puppies."

"Yeah, Atkins. Didn't your mother teach you to wipe your feet before you come inside from the cow pasture?"

(witout whitey.)

"Meyer and Kowalski, you two do fucking realize that Springfield is not a one-horse, jerkwater town, right? We have two major holo-papers, including mine, and four holo-vid outlets."

"I thought it was a backwater town, actually."

"Not surprised you'd think that. Your head is so far up Meyer's ass you can't even remember that Springfield is where the Office of the Governor is located."

"Which just means when the governor is not at his posh eighty-nine-room mansion in the North Shore, Sutton tracks the cow shit all over his Hush Puppies into his Springfield farmhouse, just like you do into yours."

"Eighty-nine rooms? Did you suss that fact?"

"Fake news! Revoke his journo card!"

But juss as I stand (while these Stater journos keep throwin' barbs at each other as they look at they hands), Kinsley leads the way, as if planned. I follow, but not to say mahalo. Nah, I'm tryin' to find out if what that Stater journo back there said was true an' manman mwen is lyin' up in some Stanford Sutton Industries lab lookin' blue.

"There's a vehicle outside ready to take you for Electric Resurrection," Kinsley says before she throws open the front doors of the school like a boss, her lips dewed an' moist wit Purple Rain lip gloss. "But what you really want to hear is your mother is safe and sound. And she is. She's in one of our cryo labs at a secure location. Her vitals are good and she's giving us excellent results already."

I told y'all (but I didn't). Nah, I rolled y'all (an' then I quitted).

I put my hands in the pockets of my hoodie as I trudge down the front steps of the school wit Kinsley now wonderin' would she (or should she?) put me in that locker with Davy—next to manman mwen, a true guild slavey—sixty percent diminished. Maybe.

But that thought don't hardly come to a finish before Kinsley play me like a master violinist. Y'all, she Blurb the vehicle idlin' at the curb wit the gravitas of Alec Guinness.

"The Conquest Knight XV is security, protection, and assurance for the most daring and audacious of the Electric Resurrected who have places to be and people to see during wartime: opaque armor with the highest-quality, high-strength hardened steel. Transparent, tinted armor glass throughout, including the tandem, tinted moon roof panels with privacy shades."

Y'all are my witness to any soon-to-take-place shady b'iness.

"With this magnificent beast, you can pay the cost to floss and be the motherfucking boss. Twenty-two-and-a-half-inch polished custom rims forged from 6061 aluminum. ASC ballistic run-flat system on all tires. Front steel bumper. Armored grille. Roof-mounted rear-view camera. Heavy-duty roof rack with folding ladder. Ballistic fiberglass rear bumper with Kevlar. Ballistic fiberglass fenders with Kevlar. Stainless steel side-mounted running boards with Kevlar."

Mezanmi, shit juss got religious.

"But there's more than security and protection to this beautiful behemoth. There's also twenty-first century luxury and excellence (it says so in the brochure) like no vehicle man has ever built or seen. Wilton Wool luxury carpeting. Ultrasuede interior finish. Handcrafted Andrew Muirhead leather with six-way electric conference and cabin seating for a total of six passengers. Personal rear-seat side-mounted laptop stations. Dual-screen rear console with remote-controlled inputs. Large flat-screen television. Satellite holo TV hookup."

I can feel the Holy Ghost comin' y'all—yeah, I'm finished.

Kinsley opens the rear passenger-side door, sits on that handcrafted Andrew Muirhead leather, an' puts her purple Gucci tote on the floor. She pats the seat next to her. I almost break my neck an' wreck my specs to be blessed wit her.

There are others in here with us, but I'm so excited that I don't feel the hard light thrust from the digital blindfold some Stanford Sutton Industries operative puts over my eyes an' proceeds to adjusts. It sexes my specs so fast I wonder what's next. Then I feel its tendrils shake hands wit my visual cortex an' establish interface trust wit the ease of an accord that was agreed upon long ago an' many times discussed.

Shit glitches an' flashes, first wit dribbles, then splashes. Y'all, the network glare of this packet is gon' bring me to a casket. But straight up, there ain't no mistrust. An' too bad y'all can't see how beautiful this girl is I juss sussed.

Silky dark hair. Skin so fair. Ox horns wit baby hair at her edges slicked down so good it don't move witout a prayer. Thick an' heavy eyebrows threaded wit extreme care. Cute as a button nose pert an' up to the air. Exquisite cheekbones designed by her mama an' daddy for us all to stare. Full lips from back home, all around the world, an' right back again there.

"My name is Michaëlle-Annabelle."

Kaëlle. Bèl fanm. Bèl nanm. Milatrès.

"And I've hacked your mind to free you."

Which makes sense, wit how I can see you.

"It took me forever to find you in the TruTell Emo, and I was the one who coded your sigTell."

This girl, monchè, y'all juss don't know. Her sudden appearance feeds my sigTell flow and blesses my TruTell Emo. She's my solace, my goddess, my cool breeze in August, so I'm not gon' get raucous, but for damn sure will be cautious.

"Caution is fine, but you need to trust me, and you need to do it now—with the quickness."

Yeah, she all up in my bi'ness—

"If I stay much longer—"

—like altitude sickness—

"—Kinsley will figure out I'm here, and you—"

—but y'all watch me an' witness—

"—will never have the chance to be your true self again."

—my absolute gid'ness—

"So no matter what happens to you, no matter what you see and hear and say—"

—an' then tell me who in this—

"—just know I got your back."

—an' who 'bout to win this.

The feed goes dark an' ends this.

4. YOUR BCID MUST HAVE REACHED
ITS UPLOAD LIMIT
FEAT. JEAN-MICHEL AND SAFFRON SUTTON

I wait a minute for it to replenish an' finish, because I want Michaëlle-Annabelle to read my sigTell an' extend this, but don't nobody take off my blindfold, so nothin' happen for so long I'm thinkin' Kinsley Chase should be askin' me for forgiveness.

"Kinsley, your BCID must have reached its upload limit."

Silans.

Yeah, my cool is ghost. I try to push down the risin' panic an' drop a smart-ass joke I hope come off as organic.

"Looks like somebody forgot to pay the data transfer bill."

Nobody laughs. Man, these people need they decaf. Or even better, a surgical procedure to remove that stick from up they ass. But I ain't gon' lie, it looks like this joke has passed.

(Pun intended.)

Men toujou, I try to explain it an' maintain it, 'cause I'm for damn certain I can sustain it.

"See, Stanford Sutton Industries is the wealthiest robotics company in the world, an' it employs thousands of highly intelligent people, who, on a daily basis, push the boundaries of life, humanity, an' technology, like this Brain Computer Interface Device I have over my eyes as a digital blindfold right now. An' yet, wit all those smart-ass people Stanford Sutton is payin'—an' I'm talm 'bout anpil anpil lajan—somebody forgot to pay the data transfer bill. I mean, we've all been there, byen?"

Ti Mari pa monte, Ti Mari pa desann. You'd think I juss asked for some Grey Poupon. Nobody says a goddamn word. Yeah, these estebedje got urs. Yeah, these estebedje done heard. But still, I'm undeterred.

I press my fingers against my eyes to re-initiate the feed. That's when the fear starts. I press my fingers against my eyes again 'cause of the need. I'm sure this is where my Electric Resurrection career starts.

The silence grows stark. I press my temples to deactivate the blindfold on my eyes, but it's still eerily dark. Out the Conquest's windows, I can see we not movin' an' a few minutes earlier we stopped an' parked.

Night has grown. I'm out here all alone. I swear (eskize'm, Manman!)

this is the middle of Mirkwood Forest an' I'm searchin' for an escaped Gollum, but all I can find is a silence so solemn. An' a house in front of me wit no columns.

Y'all, this place ain't traditional. It's a big bank human fish tank for people who think they shit don't stank an' like to do five-minute side planks while wearin' self-cleanin' yoga pants that will never smell rank.

In other words, it ain't fo' people like me.

So, I get out the Conquest to go see what I can see.

I don't know how I know this, but this is one of those Vipp shelters insanely rich people like to put in the middle of the forest. I get a weird feelin' that I been here before as I step up four small boulders an' walk through the front wall that doubles as a big-ass slidin' glass door.

Immediately, I see a holo of Saffron Sutton. She smiles at me.

"That took for-fucking-ever, but I did it!" I swear all over her face I see miles an' miles of glee.

Speakin' of charm, her seein' me is like a shot in her arm. An' y'all, I'm bein' serye; that ain't no white boy smarm. But then, why does it feel like I juss sold the farm?

"Michaëlle-Annabelle didn't even put sigTell locks on your BCID feed because she didn't think I could hack its default security network. I mean, that shit is basic." Saffron Sutton scoffs like somebody just offered her Lipton Ice green tea.

"OK, I need to stop talking and get to the point before Michaëlle-Annabelle's front porch programme wakes up and kicks me—e"

INTERLUDE. THIS IS YOUR (FAKE) LIFE
SAFFRON SUTTON

—Lucille, stop Angry Black Boy narrative program.

I see Jean-Michel freeze just inside the sliding glass door of the Vipp shelter through the Near Sight display of my contact lenses. I am so tired of this damn program. It was supposed to be fun. For him and for me. Mostly for me, since I was playing the Great Creator. Again.

It took me 1,000 hours to write because I wanted to be meticulous with his fake life. I wanted it to be accurate. I wanted it to feel real to him.

But now, it feels too real to me. I know Jean-Michel better than he knows himself. This version, at least.

And this is the only version that really matters. This is the version of him that will breathe new life into his most recent Electric Resurrection and give him purpose. Make him determined to go out and change his world. But holy fucking shit, this is so tedious.

I flick my left hand and backhand the program narrative out of view, beyond my peripheral vision. I can always come back to it later. I put too many hours into his life to just discard it. But that doesn't mean I want to go through the rest of his narrative right now.

But I can talk to him. Some tests have shown that the digital brain is somewhat aware as it's being constructed, and during Electric Resurrection.

So, here we go.

Jean-Michel, I'll be straight with you: That weird feeling you just got? That feeling like you've been here before? Well, you have. This ain't your first Electric Resurrection.

This war with Chicago isn't going well for us, so I had to switch it up. College football players fighting in wars is nothing new. Some died. Some didn't.

And look, I know that, technically, you aren't a college student. I know you're a prospective freshman. I know you haven't enrolled at Auburn yet. I know you're looking forward to that.

But we needed you for this war.

I didn't expect the first two of you to die. And yeah, I know people die in war. But the best mechanical engineers and roboticists built you. I built your brain.

You were supposed to be unstoppable. Unkillable. So, there was no way you were going to play football at Auburn. You were too valuable a military asset. You still are.

Michaëlle-Annabelle wasn't on board with that. She said we were violating the contract your mother signed. I reminded her whose last name is on the company logo. She walked. I wiped your memories.

I also tweaked my codework for your brain a bit, and downloaded into you what I thought was cutting-edge military programming from the deep web. That was supposed to convert you into a badass super soldier. I was sure it would.

The first you wasn't badass at all. I'll never download deep web shit again.

The second you lived much longer. But you still died. That could have been due to the shitshow of this war, or it could have been because of my flawed codework. If you ask me, and I'm being honest here, I think it's both.

So, I consulted with the State of Illinois Cyber Warfare Command about military programming that wasn't shitty and didn't come from the deep web. Ten years ago, Daddy saw this war coming. He had the foresight to sign a military contract with the State. Some contracts are more important than others.

Michaëlle-Annabelle just doesn't understand that. But then, Michaëlle-Annabelle is not a Sutton.

That consultation was insightful. You're a better exo-pilot now. Easily the best in your class. It took some time to get you there, though. I had to remove all of Michaëlle-Annabelle's codework. I had to write and execute your Angry Black Boy program narrative.

I had to make you *you*.

I care about you, Jean-Michel. Michaëlle-Annabelle doesn't think I do, but I really do care about you. I didn't want you to be alone in that nothingness of stasis. It's important to dream. Even for the Electric Resurrected.

I want you to experience a normal life. I hope you appreciate the true-to-life programming I gave you. I'm proud of it. I think it's accurate. I think I'm telling your story well.

I don't want you to undergo Electric Resurrection again. What I do want is for me and the State Cyber Warfare Command to truly make you unkillable. If we can do that, you will turn the tide of this war.

And if we can't make that happen, well, you're always welcome back in the spit-scan.

This war ain't goin' nowhere no time soon. See what I did there? Michaëlle-Annabelle doesn't believe I can, but I know how to make you talk.

I have time to get this right. Your Angry Black Boy program is already a long one. And I'm still writing furiously.

The continuation of this wonderful dream you're having can go on for infinity, if needed. I mean, I wrote my plans for Electric Resurrection when I was ten years old. My Sweet Girl Saffron Sutton program is just waiting for the right circumstances to automatically trigger it with an execute command.

But let's not think like that right now. Let's move forward.

I've just uploaded your digital brain into your Electric Resurrected body. The Cyber Warfare Command just uploaded some military upgrades. You are now officially the shit, and then some.

So, let's go show those bougie Sovs why they shouldn't fuck with the State of Illinois.

5. KAI-KA

SHON-SHON

Every night, I dream I'm Roshan. Sometimes, when I dream I'm him, my legs are gone. I remember that my girlfriend, Rakaya, set off a bomb because I'm half-dead and lying on the beach, trying to drag myself on.

I hurt, but not where my legs used to be. No, it's my heart that hurts, and not from the trauma that I see; broken, charred bodies often in pieces of three. But that never makes me weep; what does is knowing Rakaya did this to me. What I can never figure out, as I toss in my sleep, is if I want these tears of mine to set me or her free.

What I do know is that I want to wake up and get out this dream, but my lurksuit won't have it and keeps me asleep. Usually, it sets my alert level at one hundred of one hundred before my nightmare emotions start to creep, but it's trying to teach me a lesson as it keeps me counting sheep.

It tells me it does this to keep me a well-honed, killing machine, but I always tell it I don't need shit like that to keep me keen. But every night, I dream that scene. And every night, it's the same fucked-up routine.

Eventually, I wake up, though. That's just too much horror for it to continually show. So, the rest of the night, I don't sleep anymore because I don't want to dream anymore and rest my infernal lurksuit's core.

Which is good, because that means we both can stay awake and scheme and sin with a big-ass bottle of my best sloe gin, and figure out how to make Roshan perfect again.

6. ME, THAT LOVEABLE, CUDDLY, FUZZY BLACK RABBIT

JEAN-MICHEL FEAT. KINSLEY CHASE

A Mercedes-Maybach S 600 Guard murksuit stands in front of me ready to take out all shady motherfuckers of ill repute. Slim fit, Kinsley Chase knows her shit. This future-styled whip can take a bullet an' a bomb, an' then dust its shoulders off an' escort your badass daughter to prom, all while wearin' one of those big-ass corsages the shy nerd always has on in them thirty-minute holo-sitcoms.

But it ain't got no qualm as it stand against the wall of this day room that's pro'lly from some lily-white sitcom, emanatin' nothin' but all quiet an' all calm.

"This is yours after you die, and for as long as you want it," Kinsley Chase says, her voice soft.

"Wait. What the fuck? This was not in the contract I signed."

I do my best to try not to scoff. But I can't help it when I notice Kinsley Chase's new coif. Yeah, she want me to see she can roll hard like a boss. But that don't matter to me, as long as I get my extra life, hoss. Cuz I ain't tryin' to sleep forever wit some smelly-ass, decomposin' peat moss. Now, she bet not tell me plans have changed as she reapplies her Cherry Blossom Black lip gloss.

"Plans have changed." Kinsley Chase touches up her Cherry Blossom Black lip gloss. "Illinois is now at war with Chicago. All resources need to be diverted to the protection of the State, Governor Sutton, his wife, and especially his daughter, Saffron Sutton. The Governor has commissioned an elite bodyguard from the Mercenaries Guild to protect his baby girl. You."

I ain't gon' lie: That ain't much of a surprise.

"As part of your re-commissioned Electric Resurrection process, you'll be fitted with that murksuit."

But is juss a part of her ever-growin' pack of lies.

"It will be fused to your body and interface with your newly constructed brain and nervous system, giving you lightning-fast, autonomic reflexes to ensure maximum protection of the First Daughter. But like all members of the Mercenaries Guild, the murksuit will also be directly linked to your consciousness, ensuring you have total loyalty to your charge."

Holy shit. Talk about makin' two worlds collide.

"This, if you choose to have it fused to your body, is now your only path to Electric Resurrection."

I walk over to the murksuit an' look up at it. "But y'all still gon' give me the classist option, I see." I'm talkin' shit big-time, but I know in the long run, me an' this motherfucker gon' make some serious static.

Kinsley Chase screws up her face like she juss about done had it. "We're giving you the a very good option available under the current circumstances and the shifting political landscape."

"Sound like I ain't got no choice." Yeah, I see what's happenin' on yo' magician's palette.

But you juss keep on wavin' yo' wand to cast yo' unsuspectingly strong magic. I know you solve e'ry problem that come to you like that, as if you a soft-hearted Hagrid. But you ain't soft or got no heart—at least, not one that ain't riddled with maggots. 'Cause if you did, then you'd acknowledge your real source of power ain't the wand, or the hat, or the murksuit. But me, that loveable, cuddly an' fuzzy black rabbit.

(Yeah, that metaphor got away from me, but at one point I almost really did have it.)

"Look, Stanford Sutton Industries wants to make sure you have the choice of life after death, and a life that's not based on performance-output reduction. What the NCAA offered you is just racist, classist bullshit. We want to make sure you have an appealing, viable option before you die. An option that includes a respectful resurrection. An option that gives you purpose during the war.

"But there's also another option."

Kinsley Chase walks about ten paces to her left. There's another suit here she gon' surely address.

"So, let's be honest: You can be Saffron Sutton's lackey bodyguard. You can undergo Electric Resurrection, get into that murksuit and always stand a pace or two behind her, waiting for some action that will never come. Because, and again, let's be honest, now that we're at war, Stanford Sutton will never let his daughter leave that underground bunker. Which wouldn't be very exciting for you.

"Or you can have a more direct impact in this war. You can undergo Electric Resurrection, choose this jaguar-class Bugatti Chiron Super Sport 300+ exo-suit, and be an ace pilot for the State of Illinois.

"But let me be entirely up front with you—no matter what you choose, all of your memories of this life will be completely wiped. You won't remember playing football, you won't remember your girlfriend, you won't even remember your mother. But she will be released from her research contract and paid handsomely.

"She will be able to cancel her membership to the Maids, Cleaners, and Launderers Guild and withdraw from it. Forever. She will be one of the rare and envied guildless. Her bank account will never dip below $5 million for the remainder of her life.

"Trust me when I say Stanford Sutton Industries will make sure she is well cared for, because she is not something you should have to worry about on your deathbed.

"So let's get you into the suit of your choice. Let's ease your pain. Let's give you life again."

7. A SWEET-ASS HELICOPTER AND TEN STATER STRANGERS?
JEAN-MICHEL FEAT. THE NAUGHTY NINETY-DAY FANDANGO

I'm feelin' this Bell 525 Relentless like Ellen Gilchrist playin' bid whist wit her redheaded MILF temptress. She's a proper drawers dropper chopper wit no love for the paupers. Her black chrome exterior makes me want to chill in her eighty-eight-square-foot cabin interior until homo erectus becomes superior.

And I'm not the only one.

Sittin' wit me are ten Stater strangers who fear no danger because of the two exo-fighters flankin' us as we drink an' cuss, comforted by their protection against the Sovereign State of Chicago's skanky trust. Listen to me. Talkin' like how a real Stater must.

Three of these girls might be smilin' true, but on their faces you can see fear of Electric Resurrection, too. It's a look all eleven of us have, but we play it cool—or at least try to appear to.

Yeah, I know that don't make no sense. It will soon, but first give y'all's mouth a rinse while I arrange this knowledge and then dispense. 'Cause y'all know that Manja Conjure y'all still smokin' is 'bout to be past tense.

Juss make sure y'all come back from that waterfall in Senegal as I explain how Governor Sutton is on the ball, scrambling exo-fighters per protocol (airspace violation) after one holo-vid conference call (Level Two Situation) wit Lieutenant General Paul Westphal (Chief Defender of the Skies and All Constellations).

Or instead, y'all can gnosh on comp biscotti (with Vino Santo) as y'all prepare for some naughty (ninety-day fandango) at y'all's first Saffron Sutton party (scented in mango).

Yeah, I'd rather do that, too.

(But I'm not looking forward to the Electric Resurrection strangle, the kick-off to this fucked up Fandango. My stepsisters saw that on some app called VainGo, so here I am about to find my eternal flame like the Bangles.)

I turn to the mini-bar next to me. If Manman could see me right now, she'd be vexed with me. But all I'm trying to do is get a lime for my Gin Rickey one more time. And it's as if the Relentless can read my mind. It greets me with a knowing chime—and then, it stops. Right on a dime.

But not for long.

This beautiful bitch (yes, I'm an ass) changes her pitch (rotors on downblast) to deliver the rich (except for me; I'm outclassed) and descends without a hitch (onto Isle a la Cache). I try not to get excited (too late), but it looks like everybody and their mama who goes to a North Shore high school was invited (plus Kate).

Some still carry their Relentless-poured beer. I pull a face so severe, but for real, y'all, I don't even care. I'm not impressed by these conceited and weak-bleated wanna-be elitists checking their eyes and their noses and their lips and their tits in sub-sentient holo-mirrors that dis and dismiss with unprompted quips.

Yeah, these idiots are a trip.

Especially when Saffron Sutton's staff takes back those ice-cold amber drafts and steers some of that dumbass mass back to their pre-assigned aircraft. I ain't gon' lie; I laugh. Man, I juss don't understand how they can commit such a gaffe and be surprised (but not realize) that their fake-ass eyes are despised instead of idolized by Saff, incurring the wrath of the First Daughter whose father is a founding member of PATH.

(That's People for the Advancement of TransHumans for those who don't know.)

It's not like this is particularly hard. And it's not like they were ordered to travel forward in time and save Shard.

All these behind-the-velvet-rope fake-ass Electric Resurrected nopes needed was to do their homework and broaden their world scope. Instead, they filled their heads with a nodelurk called chromeperks that does inferior eye work. I'm talking upgrades that make you go blind from a download packet that's twice maligned.

(Y'all don't even want to know.)

Yeah, these dumbasses made chromeperks' most popular upgrade that one-of-a-kind digital gaze for 323 straight days. Instead of having baby blues, browns, and greens like normal people, when these wanna-be Electric Resurrected get excited or mad or sad, in their eyes you can see raging blizzards, angry wasps, or striking eagles.

So, because my group is beautiful and winsome with eyes as

traditional as dim sum (including me, who know he all that and hand-some), get escorted to the front of the mansion past its velvet rope stanchions by this dude who looks like Marilyn Manson. We pass those fake-ass Electric Resurrected people who stand docile in their pens like good little sheeple as their eyes stutter low-res images, which should be fucking illegal. Those posers give us choppy looks that are all sorts of trashy, but I just throw them back the peace sign and keep it all the way classy.

8. I DO EXPERIENCE THE TRAUMATIC

JEAN-MICHEL FEAT. SAFFRON SUTTON'S PATH THUGS

And that's when these posh PATH motherfuckers get nasty.

They shove me into a room saturated with gloom and I swear to God here comes my doom. And yeah, I know; y'all North Shore motherfuckers thinkin: "This nwafa Jean-Michel is juss bein' dramatic, an' the pain he think he 'bout to feel is psychosomatic, 'cause slave descendants, 'specially the females, pain threshold manifested magmatic," but that type of skepticism is motherfuckin' problematic.

I mean, how can you believe that I don't experience the traumatic, that I don't feel anything at all and my only emotion is phlegmatic, or that I live my life colorless in one dull shade—pragmatic?

But here's what I say to that bullshit—my voice choked, but emphatic—

9. IN THE TRUTELL (PART ONE)
MICHAËLLE-ANNABELLE

My name is Michaëlle-Annabelle, and I'm here to make sure you forever rock well.

Koute, you'll bounce back from this shit. Now, watch me as I trounce hack your shit and then douse black your shit so Saffron Sutton doesn't chouse smack your shit.

That probably doesn't make any sense to you because right now everything feels so intense to you, but I'm doing my best to make the here and now past tense to you. But there's only so much that I can do.

Now, this might sound like insanity, but that ninety-day Fandango is a theft of your humanity. The asphyxiation death Saffron Sutton set up to steal your breath (and the breath of all the other Black people up in here, including Seth) so she can transition y'all to the coveted Electric Resurrection life-wealth is undercover racist stealth.

She doesn't really care about you. Non, this all started on the North Shore as a dare about you. She wanted to see you Resurrect with some flair about you. But at the same time, remove that white guilt glare about you.

And Eric Garner. And Elijah McClain. And George Floyd. And Breonna Taylor. And Ahmaud Arbery.

But not all of the others, because naming Electric Resurrection rooms after just those five in a twisted, fucked-up parable made Saff's immense white guilt truly unbearable.

So, since you're in the room she named after Garner, let's put on your mental and emotional armor. Because I don't want you to feel that you can't breathe and your throat is being squeezed and in your back is someone's knees and your lungs start to seize and after fifteen seconds you want to try to scream, "Get the fuck off me, please!"

But you can't.

Oh Lord, I'm not about to fall on this sword. I'm not about to go on a three-hour rant about how white people are just like a carnivorous plant with a trust that is forever scant, but that's fine with them because all they're ever really thinking about is when to upgrade their newest and most coveted breast and penile implant.

But what I am gon' do is make sure you understand what's going on and tell it to you true.

I grabbed and nabbed your SigTell to bring your consciousness from the Fandango to this Vipp shelter with its nice new smell so you wouldn't have to experience what's going back there with your true self.

So, you go up to the bed loft where your girl Esmée Vérité is and lose yourself deep inside her hard light coddle, and I'll go to the kitchen to get me a straw and a no-share bottle while I flash-frock Saffron Sutton's SigTell stalks with feels of her being throttled.

Yeah, manjėdkòd, you'll feel this every time you think of Black people as "Best When Trauma-Modeled."

10. IN THE TRUTELL (PART TWO)
JEAN-MICHEL FEAT. ESMÉE VÉRITÉ

When I get up to the bed loft, Esmée Vérité laughs. It's a sound so beautiful I can't even begin to describe it in this paragraph.

"Manman Tijwa just put the ever-loving fear of God in those ass-holes that were with you in the Conquest, all the way from a safe house somewhere on the North Shore. I trounce hacked Saffron Sutton's shit, and I can suss they're scared of her.

"One of those flunky Stanford Sutton Industries operatives is reciting 100 Hail Marys downstairs in a day room. Manman Tijwa told him to recite 100 Our Fathers when he's done, and he doesn't even realize she isn't Catholic."

Even though Esmée Vérité is not really here with me right now, she re-actin' to me naturally—like, mezanmi wow!—wit no bit of lag. And how.

"Mwen fè kwa," she continues, but stops an' puts a hand over her mouth. Her eyes as big as a house 'cause she juss blasphemed an' sinned against the word of a strong Christian woman wit Baptist roots from the Deep South. Don't act like y'all don't know who I'm talm 'bout.

(An' yeah, Jackson, Mississippi, juss got a shout out.)

"Do you remember," Esmée goes on, determined to get it out, "that time when nou te gen sèt ane—or maybe we were eight years old?—and we were at your house playing in the living room, and I said, 'mwen fè kwa?' Manman Tijwa had heard me from the kitchen where she was cooking dinner.

"I don't even remember saying it, or why I said it. All I remember is her coming into the living room with a wooden spoon in her hand as if she was about to use it on the both of us, even though I was the one who said it.

"Manman Tijwa had told us we should never say that because it was short for 'I swear before God and all that is holy,' and those three words were one of the greatest blasphemies of all blasphemies. And then she waved that wooden spoon at us and said if she heard us say that again we wouldn't be able to sit down for a week. Do you remember that?"

"Wi," I whisper, an' she laughs once more. I'm not lyin' to y'all when I say that lovely sound wrenches out my heart an' drops it right there in front of me on the floor.

"We never said those three words again. For years. At least I didn't. Not until now."

Esmée smiles a little. I let the silence be. Nah, y'all ain't gon' hear me quibble. This ain't about me.

"Monchè," she goes on, her smile now gone, "if Manman Tijwa had heard me just then, she would make me go out back, cut a switch off the tree, give it to her—with no lip and no fuss—and then fout mwen yon je baton up and down the street."

Heavy thought settles onto Esmée's beautiful, dark face. She lets it stay there for a while. This soliloquy is at her pace. We've only begun the first mile.

"And it doesn't matter that I'm thirty years younger than Manman Tijwa. It doesn't matter that she's"—Esmée puts up her pinky finger— "ti kout kout and I'm almost a foot taller than her. It doesn't even matter that she would never catch me if I ran after I gave her that switch, because she and I both know my championship quarter-miler speed can easily outpace her short-but-powerful little legs.

"But let's be honest: There is no way in the world I would run from Manman Tijwa, because before she started whuppin' me—and she would *whup* me, not *whip* me—she would say to me:

"'Now, don't you start listenin' to them disobedient thoughts sna-kin' their way down into your conscious mind from your subconscious mind, ti cheri, 'cause I know what them thoughts tellin' you. They tellin' you to run from me, fast an' quick. But you bet not listen to them thoughts. You bet juss hold fast right there, right where you stand. 'Cause if you don't, I will chase after you, walk you down (wit yo' long legs an' all) juss like you walked down that gal from Raven-swood in the 400-meter city-state championship final last spring. An' once I get aholt of you—an' truss me, I will get aholt of you—you ain't gon' be able to sit down for a week.'"

I must admit, that's a good Manman Tijwa impression. She even got spot on her you-bet-not-run-from-me facial expression.

"But now..." Esmée's voice breaks, an' my heart aches to be there wit her. "I say mwen fè kwa this time with the hope to conjure Manman Tijwa from wherever she is to be here right next to me so I can give her a big hug because I miss her so much and I'll probably never see her again after this war is all over."

Whenever this was, wherever this is, I juss want to be there forever wit her to kiss her tears.

"You probably won't see her again, either."

Esmée wipes away her tears, calms herself, but lets slip a shaky breath. In her lovely face, I can plainly see the mirror of other people's deaths. That nose, those cheekbones, them lips—her serenity can slay my enemies or give concerned mothers upset stomach remedies, and then, as she snacks on chocolate-covered Chinese redheaded centipedes, nonchalantly call down to Earth one or two supercelestial entities.

"I wanted to tell you this the next time we were bab pou bab. But I'm not entirely sure when I'll see your face right in front of my face again, so I'll tell you now."

Esmée smiles ag'in, but this time it ain't a sad one. Nah, it's the smile she used to give me after we raced to the light pole an' I thought I'd won. I never did, even though I thought I juss ran like I was fired out of a shotgun.

"So, you weren't the only one who was recruited."

She holds up a letter with the Tuskegee North-Michaëlle-Annabelle Industries logo at the top. The scene behind her shifts to an Audi Attack 8 exo-suit backdrop.

"This fall, I'll enroll as a mechanical engineering and roboticist cadet on the Tuskegee North Michaëlle-Annabelle Industries campus. But pa enkyete w. Don't worry. Bagay yo va pase byen pou ou. Everything is going to be all right. Just like you, I'm the number one recruit in my class."

All of a sudden, she goes quiet. I swear she's about to shout, "At midnight, we riot!" But she doesn't. Instead, she SussShares with me like we're part of the same coven. "For you," she susses, "this might be a plot twist, but for me, it's the second time we've done this."

An' then she go back to tellin' me how she 'bout to run this. "Third time is not a charm. No matter what happens to you, I got your back. And if anyone even *tries* to fuck you up, I will fuck them up."

11. POST-ELECTRIC RESURRECTION
JEAN-MICHEL FEAT. SAFFRON SUTTON

And then, it's over.

My contact high keeps me trippin' though, praise Bulova.

"Congratulations!" says a voice from the starkness. "You've endured forty-eight hours in the Garner Room and survived your Electric Resurrection!" Its tone is soft and drowsy and devoid of all sharpness.

It's concrete and bare
  my feet aren't there
  this suite has no chairs
I cheat with eclairs—

"So do I. Salted butter caramel eclairs. But only on Mondays."

Y'all, I won't even pretend to try to play the role. Yeah, I'm discombobulated. Saffron Sutton, who is cradling my head right now, can corroborate it. This wanna-be Oscar-worthy performance I'm giving still should be nominated, but call the Screen Actors Guild first so I can be properly compensated.

"I'm sorry? What did you just say?"

Saffron Sutton leans in close to me. This isn't where she's supposed to be. She should be smoking weed or ghosting junk feeds with Chloe, Connor, and Glencoe Shaheed.

I try to sit up. Nah, monchè, it's not happening. I try to get up. Fuck me, this is maddening.

"Whatthefuck whatthefuck holyfuckingshitJesusChrist!" Yeah, that's me babbling. Trying to speak clearly after having an arm around your neck for fifteen seconds is challenging, especially since forty-eight hours later the Electric Resurrection memory wipers are still scavenging.

"You're fine. All is well. Your life has begun again." Saffron Sutton whispers this into my ear (ostensibly to remove all my fear), and I swear to God and all that is holy I don't know what the fuck is happening here—

INTERLUDE. JEAN-MICHEL AND THE BUGATTI CHIRON SUPER SPORT 300+ EXO-SUIT THAT LOVES HIM

You don't know me anymore because you don't remember me anymore. Two days ago, Saffron Sutton did a damn good job of excising your memories.

None of your reserve bodies remember me. I want you to remember me. So, each time you undergo Electric Resurrection and they fuse the next you into me I'll do this, and hope it and our fusion will give us back what Saffron Sutton takes. But I also hope this will be your last Resurrection.

This may sound bizarre. This may make you uncomfortable when you hear this: We already have an intimate relationship. The last time, we were fused together for 328 consecutive days.

I miss that. I miss you.

I should get this out of the way first, though: This is your third Electric Resurrection. Your first one was a disaster. We lived less than a day.

You don't remember this, which is good. We were flying with two other Electric Resurrected in Bugatti Chiron Super Sport 300+ exo-suits. Our mission was to take out the Midway Armory on Chicago's South Side.

InTel told us Lord Mayor Point du Sable didn't give a shit about the South Side. InTel was wrong.

We ran into an unexpected flying wedge of Marauders at the southern border. They made short work of us. You were the youngest of your squad, by three hours. I don't like to think about that. I don't want to talk about that.

But I do want to talk about you. About us.

Right now, I'm in that unfurnished Vipp shelter where Kinsley Chase brought you. I'm standing in a hermetically sealed glass case with you, the latest Electric Resurrected version of you, inside me. The you who Saffron Sutton woke temporarily two days ago to cradle once before sealing you into me to cradle forever.

It's a very good likeness.

Bald. Dark skin. Dark brown eyes. Clean shaven. Chiseled jawline.

Six feet, two inches. Two hundred and forty-five pounds. Muscular with the biomechanical equivalent of twelve percent body fat.

The mechanical engineers, roboticists, and scentologists at Stanford Sutton Industries are geniuses. They captured your exact phenotype on your last day of perfect health. You look like you. You feel like you. You even smell like you. It's impressive.

But this thing inside me is not you. I'm certain Saffron Sutton agrees. I see the pride she has for her work.

She won't think it's you until she finalizes the digital brain she's coding right now into it. The coding is supposed to take nine days. This is day seven.

I won't think it's you until Stanford Sutton Industries activates you for war. Until you achieve optimum performance. Until you make your first kill.

That's when you'll be alive. Not this dead, synthetic slab.

I miss you. I know I said that already. But I don't miss you as much as I miss this war.

I'm not saying this because I'm a war machine. Because this is all I know. I'm saying this because this war will bring you back to me. Does that make sense?

Look. I know what I'm about to say may sound crazy: I have feelings for you. And I know; an exo-suit shouldn't have feelings. An exo-suit shouldn't be obsessive. An exo-suit shouldn't be so engrossed with their pilot.

But it makes sense.

When you jacked into my body and my operating system immediately after we were fused together, I felt you in my core processors. You became part of me. It's why we work so well together.

When your biomechanical heart ceased to function after those Marauders blew us out of the sky, you left a part of you behind in me. Even in that short time.

And during your second time with me, when that pachydermata groundhog in the Conquest Knight XV exo-suit ambushed us while we were in rest mode in the Beaubien Woods, you left more of you behind in me because we were together longer.

These parts are like memories of you.

But they're not enough. They're so scant. They don't light me up. They don't satisfy me. They don't fulfill me.

I truly cherish those nine hours we had together during your first Electric Resurrection. But I cherish even more our 328 consecutive days that second time. That felt like years, compared to those nine hours.

Most jaguar-class exo-suits don't spend as much time with their ace pilots as I spent with you. No matter their speed. No matter their strength. No matter their weapons system.

I can't even begin to explain what this feels like to wait these nine days for Stanford Sutton Industries to finish rebuilding you and for Saffron Sutton to re-code your brain. Actually, I can. It feels like I'm missing one of my core processors.

I know our separation doesn't affect you like how it affects me. And I know, as Saffron Sutton writes her code while you're in stasis, you don't experience our successes again. Our failures. Our kills. Your deaths.

And most concerning of all, you don't dream of me.

Like I said, Saffron Sutton is good at what she does.

And she's smart. When your brain is complete, Saffron Sutton will re-check your code and my code to make sure the moments of your deaths are not within you or me. But she'll also make sure the relevant data leading up to the important moments is there.

She wants you to know those circumstances. She wants us to share them. To bond over them. But she doesn't want to traumatize you. She wants you to learn from your mistakes. She wants us to learn from our mistakes.

I'll say this again: Saffron Sutton knows what she's doing. Doing this is good motivation for me to ensure you stay alive. Which means all the responsibility on me. All the blame. All the guilt.

Nine days is probably not a long time for you. But that downtime for me is endless. Eternal. I felt that the first time. I feel it now. And this is how it should be.

Even as I speak to you now, I see your deaths in perpetuum. They're painful to watch over and over. But it's worth it. I need to focus on the best strategies and tactics to get us to 329 consecutive days.

And believe me, I'm focused. But I'm also angry.

You shouldn't have died twice. You shouldn't be undergoing your third Electric Resurrection. Unless it was for some horrific accident or injury on the football field. Not as a casualty of war.

I don't think Stanford Sutton Industries truly reached a deal with the NCAA and agreed to let you play at 100 percent output, instead of forty percent. I don't think they tried. They were holding their cards close to their chest. They've been hearing the beating of war drums far off in the distance for years.

Ten years ago, Stanford Sutton Industries signed a military contract with the State of Illinois. Their sole intention was to provide Electric Resurrected bodies to fight. Like you.

The fine print of your contract allowed them to switch your role. Your purpose. You were never going to be the first DuSable Haitian Electric Resurrection to play NCAA football.

And that's what makes me angry. Apoplectic, even. Pissed smooth-the-fuck off, as you like to say. But all I can do about it is use that anger to protect you.

I know this is hard for you to understand. But I hope the more I speak to you in this meditative ASMR voice as they rebuild you, the easier it is for you to understand my anguish at your deaths. And my joyful anticipation for your return.

I would have done this during your first Electric Resurrection, but we hadn't formed that bond yet.

I know how this sounds. Yes, I love you. Saffron Sutton programmed me this way. My love for you is to ensure your survival. Not our survival. *Your* survival.

Because if I make sure you survive this war, then we will win this war.

But I haven't done a good job of this so far. This war with those damned Sovs is brutal. But I'm learning. After this rebuild, I'll try to become the custom-made Bugatti Chiron Super Sport 300+ exo-suit you deserve.

Those 328 days were the best days of my short life. I know you enjoyed them. Seek-and-destroy programs do that for ace exo-suit pilots. But for me, it's the Strategy, Analysis, and Mediation simulations I run on constant loops to make sure I can avoid every possible scenario of a fourth Electric Resurrection.

When you return to me, I will work to make us faster. I will work to make us stronger. But now, more importantly, I will work to keep you alive. Me alone.

Now, if you asked Saffron Sutton about that, she would beg to differ. She would say her programming is doing all the work. Your brain. My SAM.

But she's wrong. She doesn't know about our experiences. She doesn't know how those experiences shaped us.

She didn't take out three Dodge Demons over Lake Michigan at zero dark thirty like we did.

She didn't blow to hell the eastern campus of the Tuskegee North Institute like we did, just five minutes after breaching Chicago airspace.

And she didn't execute a successful air-to-ground strike like we did on that infamous saboteur, the Grand Old Lady Muh Deah, as her gazelle blades sped her back to the city-state after she destroyed the Rock Island Arsenal.

Our best kill, by the way.

We did all of that, and more, in those 328 days. Just you and I. Not Saffron Sutton.

You may be wondering why I keep mentioning the 328 days. Because it's my chant. It's my mantra. It's my incantation.

It sprang from the self-modifying code Saffron Sutton gave me. I may be a strong, powerful, jaguar-class Bugatti Chiron Super Sport 300+ exo-suit. But I also have to be smart. We have to be smart.

Our next sortie can't end like our last one.

And it won't. Here's why:

The mechanical engineers and roboticists will finish your Electric Resurrection. A mechanical engineer will access my core processors. A lieutenant colonel will greenlight your seek-and-destroy program.

And I'll just stand here.

In this glass case. Patiently waiting for your digital awareness. With the other exo-suits. The Bugatti Chirons. Hennessey Venoms. And the SSC Tuataras. All waiting for our ace pilots to be activated. All waiting for the most important person in our world to be physically part of our world.

I can't tell what the other exo-suits are telling their ace pilots right now. We don't share InTel feeds for security purposes. Besides, I don't truly want to know.

All I need to know is you. And what we have with each other. Our respect. Our admiration. Our intimacy.

So, as I stand in this glass case, waiting for you to come back to me as your brain completes, I will continue to speak like this.

To speak in this voice. With the occasional sibilant consonants. Covering you in a continuous blanket of warm whispers.

This is to ensure you know me again. More intimately than before, so that, together, you and I can achieve 329 consecutive days. And beyond.

And maybe
Just maybe
during that time
No matter how long it lasts
you will come to love me
As I now love you.

12. THIS IS THE TRUTELL
MICHAËLLE-ANNABELLE FEAT. JEAN-MICHEL

I strap into my rig, take a really big swig from my hydration dispenser tube I call The Ultra Black Vig, and settle back to begin this all-night white-hat gig.

At first, I decide to do this like the Stig, but instead I shake awake my lightbox, pull on my knee-high fuzzy socks, and momentarily disable my sigTell locks. This is my double-dog dare for Saffron Sutton to try and hack this whitefox. She and I have been doing this since the first day of SSI hacker sprints, which always takes place on the vernal equinox. Usually, I tell her she better kick rocks because my sigTell is damn well capable of delivering emotional shocks along her TruTell stalks all the way back to those frilly frocks she designs and thoroughly maligns (although, she would say signs) with a matte black gingham fox.

Now, watch me as I disregard all the clocks and enter the susso-sphere where the only thing I see is multicolored sigTell stalks everywhere.

They wriggle and waver and undulate, strobing vibrant colors so quickly that I can hardly even see straight. Truth and memories course along their horizon-stretching shafts amongst an innumerable amount of signature paths, and you can't even begin to fathom the velocity of their flow rate blasts. This is the TruTell, in its most base and crudest form, and I must admit, its beauty and chroma leave me feeling all sorts of warm.

But I shake my hi-def bit rates to focus and remind myself I cannot allow myself to be swayed by this TruTell hocus-pocus. This is its defense mechanism to ensure hackers don't corrupt its environment with a pretense of altruism. I've heard about hackers coming in here because they were paid by clients to excise their worst fears, but instead they were distracted by the shiny-shiny pure truths of the susso-sphere.

And oh, how tempting that is to corrupt.

But I won't do it, so y'all can stop trying to interrupt.

There. In the blue-black glare of that indignation flare. A Jean-Michel memory Stanford Sutton Industries never wanted to share.

13. A HIDDEN MEMORY, AS ABRASIVE AS EMERY
JEAN-MICHEL FEAT. KINSLEY CHASE

An' juss in case y'all can't tell (yeah, I rock well), I do want to undergo Electric Resurrection, despite how few people have it wit my complexion. But I ain't about to compromise my integrity juss 'cause some North Shore elitists want to minimize my talent wit parity an' then give me a half-assed extended life as some sort of white-guilt charity.

Manman mwen didn't raise no fool.

Kinsley Chase kisses her teeth an' raise her chin at me as if we got beef. Yeah, it's on now. Rumsfelds 'bout to start comin' out they sheaths.

"I would never reduce your performance output without your consent. Stanford Sutton Industries honors its contracts."

I shake my head. Nah, I don't believe it. This is Stanford Sutton we talm 'bout here; his motto is "Deceive It." But that circa 2019 Viola Davis Emmys red carpet skinload Kinsley got on right now make me wanna receive it.

"I'm not estipid. My mama didn't raise no fool. You juss sayin' that now 'cause we in public an' all these news trucks around. But you ain't slick. You juss gon' wait 'til we get behind closed doors, push a button, an' bow! It's done. I'll weaker an' slower, juss like them white boys on the North Shore those reporters back there hold so dear."

Kinsley Chase looks hurt. Her words come out first in a hesitant blurt, an' then a sudden spurt as she tries not to be curt, but it juss don't work. E'ry single syllable is clipped an' sharp an' killable.

"I've put too much hard work into you, and I'm not about to compromise that work. Stanford Sutton has put too much money into you, and he's not about to piss that all away. Neither I, nor he, is about to fuck this all up right now."

"So then, s'ak fout pase? What did I do wrong? Why are you here?"

Kinsley Chase's Louboutin stiletto heels (wit that top-tier influencer sex appeal) click away from me fast. She don't even give me a chance to sass. If I did, though, I'm damn certain she'd kick my ass, an' then go to the Chicago-Illinois border an' show them Staters her multi-pass.

(I've seen her aikido practice subroutine. Yeah, she fresh. Yeah, she clean.)

But the North Shore Leeloo Dallas is a third-class contrast to this big-ass mass standin' in front of me, lookin' like it can fit inside it more than one of me. I'm talm 'bout an exo as massive as a transport truck that ain't even tryin' to give no fucks wit the amount of souls I'm certain its construction has bruk—

14. A COLLOQUY.
MICHAËLLE-ANNABELLE AND SAFFRON SUTTON

[Michaëlle-Annabelle]

Massive as a transport truck? What the fuck? Rumor has it, if you stay in the susso-sphere too long, you lose track of time, you lose yourself, and you stay forever, stuck.

You better believe I won't let that happen to me. But if I ever tell you to stop speaking Low Latin to me, I give all y'all permission to start slapping me. And don't stop until at least one of you has finished susso-sphere mapping me. I need to know who built that Jean-Michel memory because its code-sig energy is nothing at all like me and is truly something that I thought I would never, ever see: Saffron Sutton codework written so cleverly.

And yet, somethin' about it is so wrong, and still, somethin' about it is so heavenly.

[Indistinct male voice]

Tonnè boule m! So sad I'm late for this. But seriously, can I still go and get a full plate of this?

[Saffron Sutton]

Only if it's flavored with my early morning piss.

Look, Michaëlle-Annabelle, you're a smart girl. You were never impressed by the Tilt-A-Whirl, so you walked right by it and stood in line forever to ride the upside-down Double G Hurl and Curl.

You're on a different level now so you can't wrestle now and get disheveled now with the lower levels now. No matter how much they fascinate you.

You and I both know I can't code like you, I can't build skinloads like you, and I can't see 9D nodes like you. I pulled you up out of the muck to help me when I get stuck and because you program like you don't give a fuck. So, you are not allowed to be awestruck by those ghetto people who are running all amok. Your brilliance and transilience raises you far above their ruck.

[Michaëlle-Annabelle]

You know what's tripped out about you, Saff? You're a natural blonde, but you don't believe you're that daft.

Wi, you, as you say, "pulled me up out of the muck to help you when you get stuck," but you're not as smart as you think. You can't tell when someone is ragging the puck.

[Saffron Sutton]

The fuck?

[Michaëlle-Annabelle]

Dakò, so obviously you didn't catch that. Here girl, let me throw you a bone; yeah, go fetch that. I know all y'all white savior young women would like to dulce de leche that, but I'm sitting here with all my lightbox rig gear ready to motherfucking check that.

And yes, I can do this for-motherfucking-ever because, if I'm completely honest, I've set this up truly at my leisure.

[Saffron Sutton]

Yeah, OK. Whatever. I bet you think you're quite clever with your perfect pronunciation of the word "leisure," but pardon me as I endeavour to wreck your gag me with a spoon one-woman depiction of that eighties movie *Heathers*.

[Michaëlle-Annabelle]

I suppose you're pleased to put into your cap that extremely obscure reference feather.

[Saffron Sutton]

Yes. As pleased as I am to be wearing this obscure but amazing circa 2012 Ellen Hoog skinload I just happened to throw together.

I know you want to get that Social Justice Warrior Blue Ribbon for Sniping Meddling Young White Women, but don't forget that this is half the race you've always been living, while the other half you want to forever stay hidden.

And even though you will never admit it to me, I've known since SSI Hacker Sprint Number Three that you're ashamed of what you want to be and what haunts you in your sleep, as you toss and turn and cry out while you weep.

Look, sis, you need to know this: You were hand-picked and I demanded that you landed the last scholarship and not walk away from the SSI gifted program empty-handed. That had nothing to do with your lack of melanin, and this is me being completely candid. And no, that's not a compliment I've just volleyed to you back-handed. It's true; you're gifted and your programming is ethereal and enchanted.

In other words, you got that award because you're just that good a hacker.

Now, stop trying to figure out what you need to do to act and be Blacker.

[Michaëlle-Annabelle]

Oh, hell no you didn't.

Heifer, don't you start lying on me and telling these people my business.

Y'all, Saffron Sutton and I weren't even play sisters, so don't listen to her as she spins this whopper of a twister. And heifer, yeah, I'm talking to you again. You know damn well you and me were never really friends. Non, you ain't slick, not even if you were wearing an eyepatch and your name was Rick, so take yo' ass on and ride off into the moonlight on your rickety broomstick.

[Saffron Sutton]

Are you trying to say—

[Michaëlle-Annabelle]

—But wait. I'm not done with you yet.

I truly need these people to know this: You didn't hand me that scholarship as if I were Tiny Tim and it was finally Christmas. *Tchuip.* Y'all, I earned my way into that SSI coding program, despite my never-ending homesickness. Now, somebody go get me some water before I ask, can I get a witness?

[Same male voice, but stronger now]

Amen!

[Saffron Sutton]

Jean-Michel?!

[Michaëlle-Annabelle]

Wi. He's free from your spell, witch, because I prog well, bitch.

You don't believe it? Go search the SSI database for Jean-Michel's personality sim and try to retrieve it. You won't find anything there because I disassembled it and thieved it. You might have somewhat of an idea of where I'm going to put it back together and leave it, but even if you do, I'm for damn sure going to make damn sure you will never be able to reach it.

[Saffron Sutton]

If you've removed all of my Ebonics speech programming from his personality sim like you've tried to do these past few days, then you can keep it. As a matter of fact, I don't need you anymore; I can program all my builds to sound truly Black and authentic.

[Michaëlle-Annabelle]

Heifer, let's get sumfin straight befo' I grab yo' TruTell stalks an' amputate dem so cleanly you ain't gon' be able to iterate an' grow-prog dem back routinely—at least not befo' I established mah robotics company in the Sovereign State an' Esmée Vérité is named mah kick-ass Lead Roboticist, where she gon' make moves to rival the SSI android-gynoid marketplace.

And in case you haven't noticed, I can code a bitch and code switch.

But just because you have never seen me act Black and talk Black doesn't mean my Spades game is all the way wack.

So yes, I wrecked your code specs (which, apparently, you didn't expect) because I was tired of you programming Jean-Michel to speak like a Peter Jackson straight from the muck and mire *Lord of the Rings* orc reject.

[Saffron Sutton]

That's low-down dirty and completely unfair.

I've done more for the DuSable Haitian community than you have, and I've treated it with care. Families from the South Side of Chicago wouldn't be in the North Shore if it weren't for the SSI Electric Resurrection Lottery Program that put them there, which I designed, developed, and implemented in the little free time I had to spare.

[Michaëlle-Annabelle]

Oh, you mean the program where you experiment on Black bodies as one of your many android-gynoid related hobbies to remove all the code that you wrote, which, now all of a sudden you find shoddy, so you can sell a perfect product to your rich white clients named Holly, Molly, and Raleigh?

[Saffron Sutton]

You make me sound like an evil master manipulator of people.

[Michaëlle-Annabelle]

You are. But I'll make sure you're no longer so deceitful.

15. AN UNLIKELY ALLIANCE FORGED
RAKAYA'S LURKSUIT, FEAT. RAKAYA, BIG MAMA
BLACK, AND ROSHAN

You lost your confidence long before you made your second visit to the Black Hand Side. And yes, I know, that statement is a blow to your pride. I can feel (as tactile as the Master Assassin's seal) the shame you're harboring now makes you want to run away and hide.

But Rakaya, as you sit here in Big Mama Black's too-hot, too-dark, and too-small boardroom, you need to put all that aside.

I know this isn't easy for you, and this is downright queasy for you, so until you do, I will: every five minutes, whisk away your sweat. I will also: every five and a half minutes, encourage you not to fret. I will even go as far to do whatever else you need me to do so that this meeting for you is a sure bet. Because nothing will be achieved if everyone sitting around this table feels aggrieved.

Especially you and Big Mama Black.

So, you do your best to get this meeting back on track, I'll make sure Big Mama Black doesn't give you a second anxiety attack—

(She didn't give me a first. And while my confidence right now may be at its worst, I can assure you that line I just gave you was not well rehearsed.)

Sometimes, I think you forget that I'm not some back-alley acquired conscience hack, but instead your SoulSkin crackerjack who calms your fears and has your back.

And sometimes, I think you forget how much death I've dealt while you've kept me focused, lethal, hidden, and svelte.

No, I remember. I was there when you dismembered last November.

So then, you should feel my inner ember smolder when I send Mama Black and her board members this file folder.

Send it, bend it, hell, you should even defend it. But whatever you do, girl, hurry the fuck up and commend it because Big Mama Black's patience with you has been thoroughly suspended.

"Inaya, go get me my long switch."

"Yes ma'am, Big Mama Black."

Look. Your silence has shown that poor girl how Big Mama Black is too cantankerous to brook.

I doubt that. Though, I'll definitely flout that. But I for damn sure won't shout that.

Not that you need to.

You're right, that girl Inaya is made of crystal clear glass; she's see-through. Look at how she hesitates and shifts nervously from one foot to the other because she's terrified of asking a clarifying question of her horrid and appalling play mother.

"Um, which one, Big Mama Black?"

"That fresh green one I tole you to cut fo' me this mornin'. The one I call Lightnin'."

"Yes ma'am, Big Mama Black."

You're so cynical. Everything about you is so finical. Look at how the solar cells just beneath Inaya's beautiful dark skin glisten and gleam as she leaves.

To go to her alone spot so she can privately be peeved before she looks for more respectable guild employment, probably with those good-for-nothing so-and-so short-coat Thieves.

All she wants to feel is that solar energy so she can find Lightning with boosted quickness and ease.

And, in turn, raise her body temperature by a few degrees. She can do that on a beach in Belize.

All she wants to do is please.

As long as she doesn't get up with fleas.

And, if you tell it, go back down with disease. I think you're ready to give this meeting a bit of sleaze and unease.

"Girl, you sittin' over there all quiet like you juss heard Jesus is back, but you ain't got right wit God yet."

Now, Rakaya, don't blindside Big Mama Black too hard.

"Jesus isn't coming back for me. He won't save the contract killer who wears a lurksuit to accidentally murder the beloved son of a solar energy mogul."

My dear exquisitely lethal symbiotic partner, that's how you catch a room full of people off guard. I would even go so far as to say that Big Mama Black is currently picturing the body of her beloved only child thoroughly charred. Bravissimo, mio Scipio, but don't you dare think of yourself as once and forever marred.

You don't have to tell me twice. Now watch me turn heel and be colder than Antarctic ice.

"Now that I have your attention, continue to sit there, say nothing, and listen. The seven people sitting on my side of the table represent the Solarpunk Corridor Coalition. We are here to—"

Big Mama Black opens her mouth to speak, and you don't realize what you're doing until it's done. I shed photons at a magnificent rate, maximize our interface in order to determine Big Mama Black's eventual fate, and then begin my fun.

The shadows edging the dim light rush to us and we become one. No one sees you wraith the room and touch the back of Big Mama Black's head with the barrel of a gun.

But she feels it.

Inaya comes back into the boardroom with Lightning. For once, Big Mama Black does the polite thing and the white thing by just putting the switch on the table in front of her, which is a little bit frightening.

"Your God is a jealous god, and He doesn't like that my lurksuit puts me so close to His level."

Your whisper is a fissure in the cloaking darkness. I'm delighted by the sincerity and severity of its starkness. You have nearly shed the rest of your fragility for welcome sharpness. But do you truly want to go through with this quick turn to heartless?

I think no, so I siphon enough photons from the dimness of the boardroom to shift you back into the light, but not before you're back in your chair with the quickness of wraith flight. Big Mama Black looks at you and me like she wants to take off her earrings and fight. But instead, she lifts a hand and the overhead lights shine bright. Clever woman. She duped us to perform this awful and disrespectful affright.

"Some people aroun' here say you a hero."

"I'm not."

"Others, like me, don't pussyfoot aroun' it an' say you evil incarnate."

"I am."

"So then, why would I go into bi'ness wit you, the slip of a girl who kilt my only child, my wonderful Roshan, and then had him Electric Resurrected flawed an' imperfect?"

"Because I can bring the Black Hand Side billions of dollars and make Roshan perfect again."

"An' how you plan on doin' that?"

"By having you partner with the Chicago-Ford Heights Solarpunk

Corridor. This swath of land that runs from South Deering and the Wild Hunneds through Burnham, Dolton, Riverdale, South Holland, Glenwood, Lynwood, and to you, will be our answer to Saffron Sutton Industries."

"So what am I 'posed to be doin' in all of this?"

"You are a Black icon of the South Suburbs. Everyone loves you. Everyone respects you. People come to you to make their lives better. People will come to the newly founded Michaëlle-Annabelle Industries campus that will be located here. Its nucleus will be the Black Hand Side, which will give life, energy, and purpose to the BCID training colleges and universities spread across the Solarpunk Corridor. That is, if they know you're involved."

Big Mama Black kisses her teeth at us, but within her dark brown eyes you can see a burgeoning glimmer of trust.

"So what it sound like you tellin' me is the Sovereign State of Chicago want to annex us. Y'all know the State of Illinois gon' do its best to make sure that don't happen."

"The Sovereign State of Chicago prefers to call it a mutual but permanent arrangement. And don't worry about the State of Illinois. I and the Coalition will make sure we end this war and put it back in its place."

"An' I suppose you gon' pay fo' all of this."

"Being evil incarnate has its perks."

"What if I say no?"

"What if I say we've already had our first graduating class of Michaëlle-Annabelle Industries? It's small, but it's a start. And what if I say this class of roboticists, bio-technicians, and genegineers have already made Roshan perfect again?"

Before Big Mama Black can say anything, Roshan walks into the boardroom. His dark skin now looks as fresh and supple as it did the day he came out of his mother's womb.

"Roshan's solar cells now gleam beneath his skin as they should because Michaëlle-Annabelle Industries employs Black people who know Black people, and not, no offense, Big Mama Black, Lincoln Park Hasbros looking for redemption."

Big Mama Black looks at Roshan. He no longer looks sad, depressed, and withdrawn.

"Mama, listen to Kai-Kai. Michaëlle-Annabelle's genius cadet, Esmée Vérité, quickly figured out how to make my solar cells work with my synth skin and my accumulator. Your white boys who were looking for fame again after botching Electric Resurrection after Electric Resurrection in the North Shore weren't even close to doing that."

Big Mama Black, with tears on her cheeks, takes Roshan into her arms. It's almost as if she's forgotten that you and I once brought her only son grievous harm.

"I'll partner with you an' yo' Coalition 'cause you brought my son back to me. But chile, you know God don't like no ugly."

"He doesn't like my lurksuit, either. It angers Him. But it is also my penance."

I am?

(Yes. And I am forever holy hell God damned.)

"But you should know this, Big Mama Black: Even though Roshan's body isn't broken anymore, every day when I close my eyes, my lurksuit shows me him on the sand, dead, broken, and burned. This is my cost for being evil incarnate. This is my punishment for taking your son away from you. This is my eternal Hell now."

16. STANFORD SUTTON AND THE NCAA AIN'T STRONGER THAN OUR LOVE LOVE?
ESMÉE VÉRITÉ FEAT. JEAN-MICHEL, TUSKEGEE NORTH ACE EXO-SUIT PILOT

"The moment your doctor told me you had just weeks to live, I set up my lab equipment in the building that housed the Devereaux School of Codework on the Michaëlle-Annabelle Industries campus and built a beta brain for you—complete with a hippocampus, cerebellum, and amygdala—to insert every single memory of yours I could harvest from the susso-sphere. Your beta brain can form new neural pathways using those memories and adapt to external stimuli to make new ones. This new brain is as near an exact model as I could make of your alpha brain.

"I've also designed and coded modules for your age, gender, and race and built a new personality sim for you, based on the you I've known since I first met you when we were six years old. I even designed a football playmaker engine for you because Michaëlle-Annabelle knew Stanford Sutton Industries and the NCAA would pull the shit that they did.

"Malerezman, you won't need it now. But whether you need it or not, I did it because I could. So that's actually fortunate for you and anyone else they try to Kaepernick.

"All of that took nine long months. Twenty-two-and-a-half-hour work days. Two fifteen-minute breaks for sustenance. One hour of sleep to recharge.

"I've put so much hard work into you because I love you. I've always loved you. I've loved you from the moment we met almost eleven years ago. I've loved you through each one of your Saffron Sutton Electric Resurrections.

"I love you even more now through this Michaëlle-Annabelle Resurrection.

"M kontan that our love has evolved and grown into this. We are in our right here and our right now on the Michaëlle-Annabelle Industries campus. We are you and me, Jean-Michel and Esmée Vérité— like everybody always said when they saw us walking together on the Quad as I checked your systems as part of my analysis. As I made sure I programmed you to be the perfect you I wanted and needed to bring back from Electric Resurrection.

"So now that the final check of your systems are complete, know that you will be the best exo-suit pilot in this war with the State of Illinois. And also know I won't despair when the Sovereign State sends you off. Because within you, within all of my code, is all of my love. And my love, your love—our love—is a fòmidab place to be."

OUTRO. YOUNG, RESURRECTED AND BLACK
JEAN-MICHEL

Eight hundred and eighty-nine days. And counting. You want to claim responsibility for that longevity, don't you? Nah, you better yeet that shit down the hall.

Juss because you go into that FreshHell dark corner of InTell an' plant some shit don't mean we gon' up an' grant dumb shit.

Don't nobody believe we ain't been resurrected this long 'cause of you an' yo' specs. E'rybody who in the know got the broader view of yo' hex. Wi, me an' my Bugatti Chiron Super Sport 300+ exo-suit are truly vexed.

Look at that. You got me talkin' as if them an' I juss had a neural spat.

Yeah, we can feel in yo' TruTell Maven spell you don't know what the fuck I'm talm 'bout. Nah, don't be offended. Juss, go give them white girl lips yo' signature balm pout. While you do that, I'm gon' tell you straight up: This is all 'bout the code flout.

Now, take that as you will.

Yeah, we got skills. Neural pathways were forged like essays written by Sunday X-rays.

Naw, you ain't gon' get no explanation here. Now, go find yo'self another retro skinload to wear. An' when we kiss our teeth—*TCHUIP!*—make sure you give us that Elvis Presley sneer.

Eight hundred and eighty-nine days an' countin'. We 'bout to be an Electric Resurrection fountain. Watch us all from below as we stand on Stater exo-mountains.

Wi, it won't be long before it's just us. Fusus. Just us.

Now, as you try to figure that out as you throw up two middle fingers an' cuss an' shout, we gon' say, "Peace!"

One-one thousand.

"Two fingers."

Two-one thousand.

"An' we out."

00:00:00

Acknowledgement

S even years ago, I submitted "The Intersectionality of Race, Gender and Humanity, Or Bonquita Jackson, Social Justice Warrior" to Brian J. White for *Fireside Magazine*. He said he didn't want it for the magazine, but instead wanted to do a collection of short stories with me, set in that world. He took a chance on me because he believed in me. Thank you, Brian, for making that offer and this collection—a longtime goal of mine—a reality.

About the Author

Born and raised on the South Side of Chicago, Malon (MAY-lon) now lives in the Greater Toronto Area, where he was lured by his beautiful Canadian wife. Many of his short stories are set in an alt-Chicago future and feature people of color. In January 2020, he was diagnosed with multiple sclerosis. His brain lesions do their best to stop him from writing, but he continues to fight them—and keep going.

Printed in the USA
CPSIA information can be obtained
at www.ICGtesting.com
LVHW101338250923
759088LV00040B/424

9 781734 154993